The BIG NIGHT NIGHT Book

THE BODLEY HEAD
LONDON

1 3 5 7 9 10 8 6 4 2

Night Night Sleep Tight first published in the United Kingdom by The Bodley Head Children's Books 1998
Sweet Dreams first published in the United Kingdom by The Bodley Head Children's Books 2001
Cuddle Up Tight first published in the United Kingdom by The Bodley Head Children's Books 1999

This edition first published by The Bodley Head Children's Books 2001
A division of The Random House Group Ltd
London Melbourne Sydney Auckland
Johannesburg and agencies throughout the world

Printed in Singapore

THE RANDOM HOUSE GROUP Limited Reg. No. 954009

www.randomhouse.co.uk

ISBN 0 370 32725 X

CONTENTS

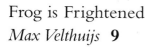

FROG IS FRIGHTENED

Max Velthuijs

Frog was very frightened. He was lying in bed, and
he could hear strange noises everywhere. There was
a creaking in the cupboard and a rustling under the
floorboards.

"Somebody is under my bed," thought Frog.
He jumped out of bed and ran through the dark
woods until he reached Duck's house.

"How nice of you to come and see me," said Duck.
"But it is rather late. I'm about to go to bed."

"Please, Duck," said Frog. "I'm frightened. There's a ghost under my bed."

"Nonsense," laughed Duck. "There's no such thing."

"There is," said Frog. "The woods are haunted as well."

"Don't be frightened," said Duck. "You can stay with me. I'm not afraid."

And they huddled into bed together. Frog cuddled
Duck's warm body and wasn't frightened any more.
All of a sudden they heard a scratching noise on the
roof.
"What was that?" asked Duck, sitting up with a jolt.
The next moment they heard a creaking on the stairs.
"This house is haunted too!" shouted Frog. "Let's get
out of here."
And they ran out into the woods. Frog and Duck ran
as fast as they could. They felt there were ghosts and
scary monsters everywhere.

Eventually they reached Pig's house and, gasping for breath, they hammered on the door.
"Who is it?" asked a sleepy voice.
"Please, Pig, open the door. It's us," shouted Frog and Duck.
"What's the matter?" asked Pig angrily. "Why have you woken me up in the middle of the night?"

"Please help us," said Duck. "We're terrified. The woods are full of ghosts and monsters."
Pig laughed. "What nonsense. Ghosts and monsters don't exist. You know that."
"Well, look for yourself," said Frog.

Pig looked out of the window, but he couldn't see anything unusual. "Please, Pig, may we sleep here? We're so scared."
"OK," said Pig. "My bed is big enough. And I am never frightened. I don't believe in all that rubbish."

So there they were, all three of
them together in Pig's bed.
"This is nice," thought Frog.
"Nothing can happen now."
But they couldn't sleep. They
listened to all the strange,
frightening noises in the woods.
This time, Pig heard them too!
But luckily the three friends
could comfort each other. They
shouted out that they were not
scared – that they weren't afraid
of anything. Eventually they fell
asleep, exhausted.

Next morning, Hare went to visit
Frog. The door was wide open and
Frog was nowhere to be seen.
"This is strange," thought Hare.
Duck's house was also empty.
"Duck, Duck, where are you?"
shouted Hare. But there was no
answer. Hare was very worried.
He thought something terrible
must have happened.
Terrified, he ran through the
woods looking for Frog and Duck.
He looked and looked but there
was no trace of his friends.

"Perhaps Pig will know where they are," he thought.
Hare knocked on Pig's door. There was no answer.
It was very quiet. He looked in through the window
and there he saw his three friends lying in bed, fast
asleep. It was ten o'clock in the morning! Hare
knocked on the window.
"Help! A ghost!" shouted the three friends.
Then they saw that it was Hare.

Pig unlocked the door and they all ran outside.
"Oh, Hare," they said. "We were so frightened.
The wood is full of ghosts and scary monsters."
"Ghosts and monsters?" said Hare, surprised.
"They don't exist."
"How do you know?" said Frog angrily. "There
was one under my bed."
"Did you see it?" asked Hare quietly.
"Well, no," said Frog. He hadn't *seen* it but he
had heard it.
They talked about ghosts and monsters and other
ghastly things for a long time.

Pig made some breakfast.

"You know," said Hare. "Everyone is frightened sometimes."

"Even you?" asked Frog, surprised.

"Oh yes," said Hare. "I was very frightened this morning when I thought you were lost."

There was a silence.
Then everyone laughed.
"Don't be ridiculous, Hare," said Frog.
 "You have nothing to fear. We are always here."

ONE ROUND MOON AND A STAR FOR ME

Ingrid Mennen and Niki Daly

One round moon.
So many stars.
A falling star, Mama!
Look how Papa catches it in his warm brown blanket.
See how it slips into his silver milk bucket.
"A star for a new baby," says Mama.
Now, Moon, please go! Go to your home.
Go to sleep in your hut. Roll up night.

Look how Sun is chasing
Moon, Mama.
Big round moon, back to her
empty hut.
Ah! There! One round sun!
Hurry through the grass – make
it gold. Run over the hill, past
Papa's herd.
Come, Sun, here!
Come warm our home.
For there's a brand new baby in
our hut today.

Makazi – my aunty – lifts me high. I stick two stalks of sun-yellow grass in the roof, above the door.

Makazi says, "Now the men will come in only when the inkaba-cord falls from the baby's belly." Nomsa, Sindi and Nono bring water for the baby, balancing buckets on their heads.

Sis Beauty brings a new cake of soap she has saved for so long. Sis Anna brings a little paraffin lamp made from a tin and a piece of wick-cloth to light for the baby. Gogo - our grandmother - and her friends bring fresh cow-dung for a new floor. Inside, Mama sings a tula-tula hush-hush song to the baby. And then Papa comes. He leaves his silver bucket, brimming with milk, at the door and kneels to look at the baby's two tiny hands.

"They look like my hands," he
says.
He looks at the baby's tiny round
ears. "Mama's ears."
He unwraps the blanket, and
there are two small feet with ten
tiny toes.
"They will walk well." Papa nods.
"I'm the baby's father," says Papa
with a smile.
We walk to the other men, but
my heart feels dark, like a night
with no moon.

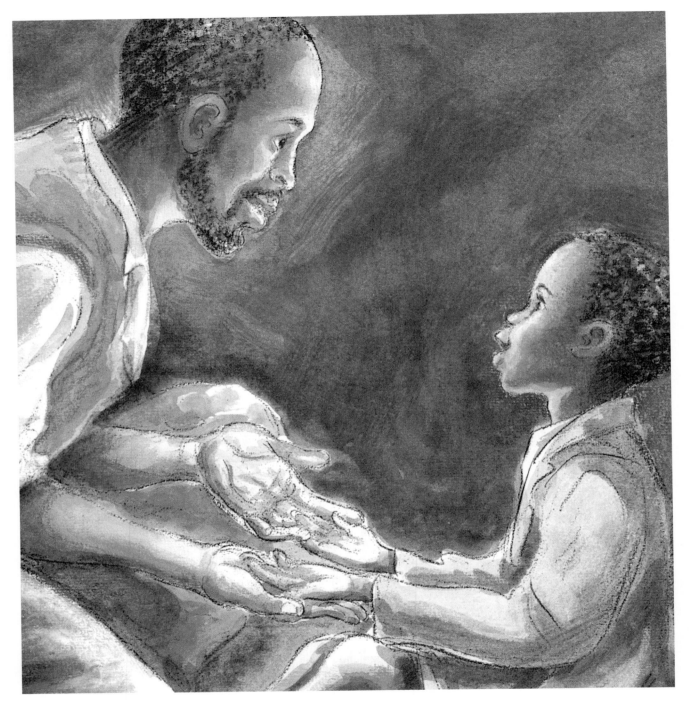

At last I ask, "Papa, are you really my papa too?"
He takes my hands and puts them next to his. "See," he says.
"I am really your papa too."
He looks me close in the eye. "Your eyes are like Mama's eyes.
You are your papa's child and you are your mama's child."

He puts his arms around me and says, "Tonight, when the moon is big and round and the stars light up God's great sky, I'll show you, there is also a star for you."

One round moon.
And a star for me.

⋆ RABBIT MAGIC ⋆
Susie Jenkin-Pearce
and Julia Malim

November grey, end of day.
Mist time,
    smoke time,
        rabbit time,

        magic time.

Small boy follows through the
gate. Golden time, berry time,
crimson leaves in the lake.
Footsteps follow, join the chase.
Where to? Where next?
Look around.
What's hiding there in autumn
leaves and evening light?

The moon shines down
as secret friends dance
on into the night.

Follow rabbit through his door,
time is passing into sleep.
Falling snow, winter time,
peaceful snow, feather soft.

Spring sun shines and small
boy wakes, follow rabbit,
flutter wings.
Buds unfurl and thrush sings
sweet, the season's green, the
blossom's pink.

Small boy follows through
the arch, to gold and blue.
The spring has passed.
Silent heat and poppy red,
a summer's beauty will not last.

Danger, rabbit! Race through seasons.
Follow small boy back to safety,

back to mist and bonfire burning,
frosty air and warm soft bed.

November grey, end of day.
Mist time, smoke time, rabbit time,

magic time.

TIMID TIM AND THE CUGGY THIEF

John Prater

Tim was a shy little boy.
He wasn't very brave, and didn't like noisy,
messy fun or being splashed or rough
and tumbles. He didn't like big adventures.

He only wanted to be still and quiet, with his special soft and sleepy blanket, his cuggy.
He took his cuggy everywhere, and kept it close by him always.
The other children would sometimes tease him by singing the CUGGY THIEF SONG!

Look out! Beware the cuggy thief
Who creeps around at night,
And steals away your favourite things
If you don't hug them tight!
They say he can be frightened off
If you put up a fight!
But none of us would ever dare
Face such an awful sight.

One dark and windy night, Tim lay in bed, holding his cuggy tight. But when he fell asleep, he tossed and turned – and let it go!

A chilling blast of air blew through the bedroom, and Tim awoke to find his cuggy gone. He let out a little cry, which grew bigger, and bigger, and bigger... until he yelled at the top of his voice, "Come back, you thief! You rascal! Give me back my cuggy!"

Tim leapt out into the night to catch the thief.

The streets were dark and empty.

The wood was darker still.

The path was steep, the mud was deep, and though his heart beat fast,

Tim never took his eyes off the wicked rogue ahead.

The weather grew wild, and the waves crashed loud.

But Tim bravely kept going on. He knew that he was getting close to the cuggy thief's dreadful lair.

He took a deep breath, then boldly entered the dim and rocky hole.

"Give me back my cuggy," he yelled.

Tim grabbed his cuggy.

"It's mine," he shouted.

The startled cuggy thief grew bigger, and bigger, and bigger, let out a horrid scream, and turned to pounce...

But Tim did not run. He stood quite still, and faced that awful sight.

The horrid scream grew faint until it was no more than the distant whistling of the wind. His huge darkness grew pale and thin, until it was no more than the smoke curling from the fire.

"Phew!" said Tim. "Serves you right." He knew there was nothing left of that horrid villain. The cuggy thief was gone for ever.

Tim gathered together all the cuggies, teddies and best-loved toys in the wicked robber's hoard.

The boat was full for the journey home.

Everyone cheered the hero Tim
for being the bravest boy ever.

But even the bravest boy ever still cuddled cuggy
for just a little longer.

☆ BEDTIME ☆
Tony Ross

Time for your bath.

But I'm not dirty yet.

That's

better.

Time for your bath.

I'd rather wash my hands.

I'd rather wash my face.

I'd rather clean my teeth.

I'd rather brush my hair.

Oooh! I don't want a bath.

I'd rather go to bed.

Why?

There's a spider in the bath

... and Ted's in bed.

✦ Burning ✦
the Tree
Shirley Hughes

William and Grandpa were taking down the tree. Christmas was over and it was time to put all the decorations away in the loft until next year. Grandpa pulled off the shiny glass balls and handed them to William who laid them carefully in their box. They took down the tinsel and unwound the fairy lights.

Then they wrapped the two little glass birds and the angel with golden wings in tissue paper and put them away too.

When they had finished, the tree looked rather bald and old without its sparkle. The presents which had been stacked underneath its boughs had all been opened on Christmas day, of course. And it no longer smelt of that wonderful foresty green smell as it had when they bought it. It leaned sideways in its pot. A lot of needles came off and scattered on the carpet.

"What a mess!" said Mum. "I'll never get them all up. You'd better move it out of the way, you two." And she briskly plugged in the vacuum cleaner. Vacuuming always put her in a bossy mood.

William and Grandpa laid the Christmas tree in a dust sheet and dragged it as far as the back door, trying not to leave a trail of pine needles behind them.

"Get your coat. We'll have a bonfire," said Grandpa.

William found his coat. Then he followed Grandpa to the door of his room and waited while he looked for his old gardening jacket.

Grandpa had not lived at William's house for very long, only since Gran had died. He had his own room and his own television set. It was quite a small room and it was very full of things.

There were some photographs on the mantel shelf, one of Gran and Grandpa on their wedding day, one of Mum when she was a baby and one of Grandpa's football team. Grandpa was right in the middle, holding the ball, because he was the goalkeeper.

William spent a lot of time in Grandpa's room. Sometimes they watched television and sometimes they just chatted. William loved hearing about all the adventures Grandpa had had when he was a young man, and looking at his things. There was one special box, a polished wooden one with brass handles, which stood on the high shelf above the books. Grandpa never showed anyone what was in there.

But William had seen inside the box. He had peeped into it one day when Grandpa was out. He just couldn't resist the temptation.

It was a sad disappointment. There was nothing interesting to see, only some boring old letters, a train ticket, a few pressed flowers and some papers which looked like poems but the writing was too difficult for William to read. Afterwards William felt miserable and uncomfortable when he looked at the box. He felt bad about knowing what was in there when Grandpa didn't know he knew. He tried hard to forget all about it.

It was nearly dark when they went outside, with only a streak of red left in the sky. William and Grandpa dragged the tree down to the rubbish heap at the bottom of the garden. It was Grandpa's special place behind the greenhouse by the end wall. He spent a lot of time there, piling up leaves and garden rubbish. Then he would lean on his rake and light his pipe. Mum didn't like Grandpa to smoke indoors. She said she couldn't stand the smell.

They heaved the tree on to the big pile of leaves and twigs
which was already there. Its bare arms stuck up bravely into the sky.

Grandpa went indoors again and fetched out a big bag full of old
paper chains and dry holly which had decorated the hall. He packed
them round the tree. Then he pulled out his matches and set light
to them.

"This will make a grand blaze," he told William. The paper and holly caught at once and burned brightly. Then they flared into white ash and the twigs and leaves started to smoulder and crackle and give off smoke. Flames began to lick through them, small at first, creeping up towards the tree. When they reached the dry pine needles the whole thing suddenly took fire.

Flames shot up with great eddies of smoke. The Christmas tree branches were all at once bright and glowing, covered with festive sparks. As William watched, the wall behind him seemed to melt and quiver. His eyes were watering, but the smell was wonderful. They stood and looked at the fire for a long time. They watched until at last the tree burned out and collapsed into the pits and caves of ash.

Then Mum called William indoors. He left Grandpa standing there, staring into the fire.

Later, when it was quite dark, Grandpa was still out there. They could see the red glow at the bottom of the garden.

"Supper will be ready in ten minutes," said Mum, as she drew the curtains. "Run and tell him, will you, William?"

64

William put on his coat again and ran down the garden path. Grandpa was standing exactly where he had left him. But he had something under his arm. It was the box with brass handles.

"Let's have one more good blaze before bedtime," said Grandpa as William joined him. And then he opened the box and flung all the letters and things that were inside on to the bonfire. Just like that! They caught alight instantly, and once again the cheerful flames leapt up.

"But I thought they were special," said William as they watched them burn.

"They were," said Grandpa, "but it's not things that are important really. The special things are in my head. And my heart. So why not get rid of the rest?"

William had never heard Grandpa say anything like that before. He didn't quite know how to answer. He took Grandpa's hand and stood leaning up against him until the flames died down and were finally gone.

"I looked into your box once," said William.

"That's all right. You were welcome," said Grandpa. "They made a grand blaze, didn't they?" he added, after a pause.

William suddenly felt happy. "Mum says I can stay up a bit and watch the football on television, as it's Saturday," he told Grandpa. "Will you watch it with me?"

"You bet I will!" said Grandpa. "You run along and tell Mum I'll be in just as soon as I've finished this pipe."

☆ DAD! I CAN'T SLEEP ☆
Michael Foreman

Little Panda couldn't sleep.

"Mum!" he called. "Can I have a drink?"

Mum said, "It's your turn, Dad. I've done enough today."

Dad took Little Panda a drink, kissed him goodnight and went downstairs.

"Dad!" called Little Panda. "I still can't sleep. Can I have another drink?"

"No," said Dad. "Go to sleep."

"I can't," said Little Panda.

"Count sheep," said Dad. "Then you'll go to sleep."

"How?" said Little Panda.

Dad climbed the stairs and sat on Little Panda's bed.

"How do I count sheep, Dad?" asked Little Panda.

"Just close your eyes," said Dad. "Now imagine sheep jumping over a fence. Count them as they jump. One. Two. Three. Four. Five. Six. Then you will fall asleep."

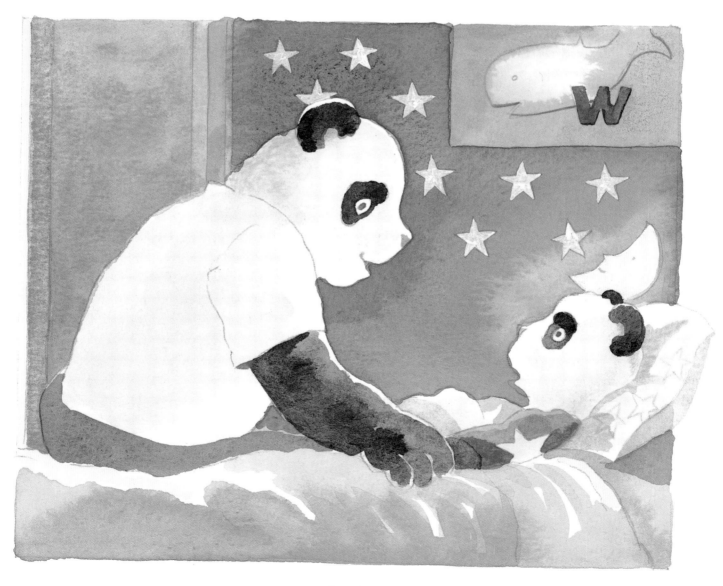

Little Panda closed his eyes
and counted sheep.
"One. Two. Three. Four. Five
and a lamb. Six. Seven and
another lamb..."
Quietly, Dad went downstairs.

"Dad!" called Little Panda.
"I can't sleep."
"Count sheep!" called Dad.
"I've done that and I still can't sleep," called Little Panda.
"Count something else," shouted Dad. "Count cows!"
Little Panda closed his eyes and counted cows.
"One. Two. Three. Four. Five. Six. Seven. Eight. Nine. Dad! I still can't sleep."

"I am not coming up again!" shouted Dad. "Count pigs or tigers!"
Little Panda counted tigers.
"Sixteen. Seventeen. Eighteen. Nineteen tigers and three little pigs. Dad! I still can't sleep."
"Count elephants! And I don't want to hear from you again," shouted Dad.
Little Panda counted elephants.
"Forty-six. Forty-seven. Forty-eight. Forty-nine."

Then he counted rhinos and hippos,
giraffes and polar bears, and still he
couldn't sleep.
"Dad! I've counted all sorts of things
and I still can't sleep."

"Dinosaurs!" shouted Dad. "Have you counted
dinosaurs?"

"No," said Little Panda.

"Well, count dinosaurs. And you know there are lots of
different kinds. Make sure you count all of them.
AND GO TO SLEEP!"

Little Panda started to count dinosaurs.

"Two hundred and two diplodocuses. Two hundred and
three diplodocuses. Two hundred and four diplodocuses.
Forty-six stegosauruses. Forty-seven stegosauruses..."

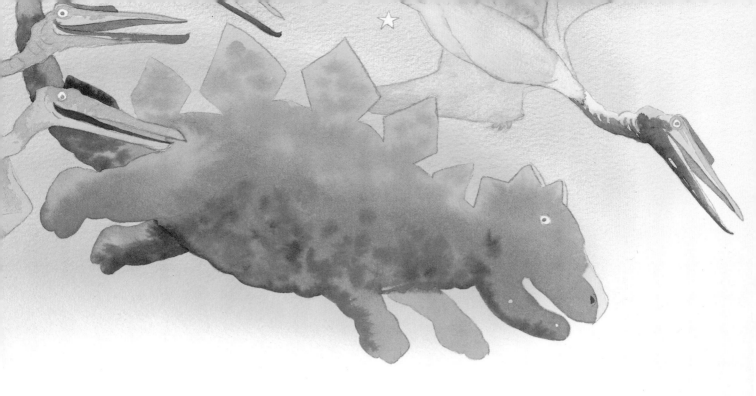

But still Little Panda couldn't sleep.
"Two zillion pterodactyls. Two zillion and one
pterodactyls. Two zillion and... Dad! Dad!"
"What is it now?" yelled Dad, as
he threw the laundry at the cat
and stomped up the stairs.
He pushed open Little
Panda's door.

I WANT TO SEE THE MOON

Louis Baum and Niki Daly

Toby woke up in the middle of the night.

"Daddy," he called, "Daddy."

Toby listened as Daddy's footsteps came up the stairs.

"Hello, Toby!" said Daddy, as he lifted Toby in his arms.

"I want to see the moon," said Toby.

"Would you like to make a wee first?" asked Daddy.

"Yes," said Toby.

They went to the bathroom.

"I want to see the moon," said Toby.

"Now let's put on a clean nappy," said Daddy.
"I want to see the moon," said Toby.
Daddy filled a glass of water for Toby.
"I want to see the moon," said Toby.
"Let's go downstairs for a little while," said Daddy.
"I'll give you a piggyback."
"I want to see the moon," said Toby.

In front of the fire was Toby's favourite book, still
open where he had left it.
"Let's read a story," said Daddy.
"I want to see the moon," said Toby.
Under the kitchen table were Toby's building bricks,
just where he had left them.
"Let's build a castle," said Daddy, "a big castle with
chimneys and windows and turrets and things."
"I want to see the moon," said Toby.

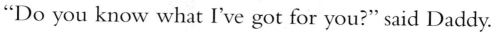

"Do you know what I've got for you?" said Daddy.
"A lovely mug of warm milk."
"I don't want a lovely mug of warm milk," said Toby.
"I know what you want," said Daddy, "you want to see the moon."
"Yes, please, I want to see the moon," said Toby.
So they went outside, into the garden, to look at the moon...

But the moon wasn't there.
There was nothing in the sky but big black clouds.
But a little wind was blowing.
It was blowing the big black clouds across the sky.
Every now and then a little light from the moon shone through.
The moon was playing hide-and-seek behind the clouds.

"Where's the moon, Daddy?" asked Toby.
"Ssh," said Daddy. "If we wait here a little while and watch very closely, the wind will blow the clouds across the sky until the moon breaks through the clouds and –"

"There's the moon!" said Toby.
"It's a beautiful moon," said Daddy.
"Beautiful moon," said Toby.

"Goodnight, moon," said Toby.

SOMEONE SOMEWHERE

Henrietta Branford and Lesley Harker

There was once a child who never knew her mother. Well, perhaps she did when she was very little. But time passed, she did not see her any more, and slowly she forgot her.

She was brought up by a nurse who made her wash her hands and brush her hair and eat cabbage and change her socks and go to bed at bedtime.

The nurse taught her everything she needed to know, especially all the things she must never do. "Promise me," she said, "NEVER to play in the deep, dark forest."

"Why not?" asked the child.

"Because nobody knows what's in there," said the nurse. And that, she thought, was that.

But it wasn't.

Time passed and the child forgot her mother's face, her voice, the smell of her skin, and how she used to sing at night. And the more she forgot her, the more she missed her, until one day she could bear it no longer.

The child remembered her nurse's warning: nobody knows what's in the forest.

But then, she thought, nobody knows what isn't. Maybe all that I have lost is in there.

And off she went to find out.

She came to the edge of the town and there beyond lay the deep, dark forest. And in she went, and on she went, and the trees grew thick about her, and she began to feel afraid.

Wouldn't you?

"Hello?" called the child. "Is anybody there?"

Nobody seemed to be, and she walked on.

Presently she met an old woman.

"What are you doing alone in the forest?" asked the old woman.

"Looking for something," said the child.

"What are you looking for?" asked the old woman.

The child shook her head. She couldn't remember what she was looking for. She only knew that it was something nice, and she wanted it.

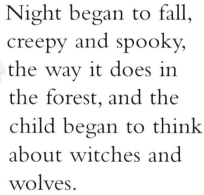

"Never mind," said the old woman. "I want a child to fetch my firewood and trim my toenails and catch my cat and dish up my dinner. You'll do."

"No I won't!" said the child, and she ran off under the treees.

Night began to fall, creepy and spooky, the way it does in the forest, and the child began to think about witches and wolves.

"I wish I had stayed with my nurse," she said. But deep in her heart she was glad that she hadn't. So she climbed a tree, wrapped herself in her blanket, and went to sleep.

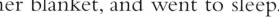

In the morning things looked better, and she went on her way.

She came to a little hut in a clearing and outside on a rickety bench there sat a woodman.

"What are you doing in the forest?" asked the woodman.

"Looking for something," said the child.

"What are you looking for?" asked the woodman.

The child shook her head. She couldn't remember what she was looking for. She knew only that it was something nice, and she wanted it.

"Don't go," said the woodman. "Stay here with me."

"No!" said the child. "I would rather be lonely on my own until I find what I am looking for."

On she went, until she came to a
dark river winding through the forest.
The river turned around a pile of
rocks and spread itself into a
deep, still pool.

A boat bobbed on the water
and a woman waved at her.
"Come over," she called.
"Come to lunch!"
"Thank you, I will," called the
child, and she climbed into a rowing boat.

"We're sailing on down river after
lunch," the woman said. "Will
you give up your search and
come with us?"

"No," said the child, "I
cannot."

Night fell, and with it
fell the first snow of winter.

Snow's early, thought the
child. I must find shelter for
tonight.

She looked around, and off in the distance she saw a most peculiar sight. A big old hollow log lay on its side, half buried in glistening snow. From out of each end of the hollow log blew plumes of steam. As she grew nearer to the log the child heard a deep rumbling grumble which came and went with the plumes of steam.

"Thank goodness I brought my torch," she said to herself, and she bent down and shone a beam of yellow light into the hollow log. Inside the log the child saw one of the most comfortable and comforting sights she had ever seen.

There was a mother bear, and a father bear, and three cubs, all curled and cuddled and cossetted around each other in a great furry heap of steam-breathing, rumble-grumbling, sleepy-winter-hibernation-bearfulness.

"Mother!" she whispered. "I've found you! Can I come in?"

Deep in her winter sleep, the mother bear heard the child. "Of course you can," she growled.

So the child crawled into the hollow log and settled herself comfortably against the big velvet stomach of the mother bear, and there she stayed all winter.

Spring came to the forest around April. Suddenly the winter was past, flowers appeared and the birds sang from dawn till dusk.

The bears stretched, and breathed deep, and scratched six months' worth of itches.

The cubs looked out of the hollow log at the greening forest. They heard birds singing and bees buzzing and they scrambled to their feet and set off to explore the woods.

Father Bear looked at Mother Bear. "How about a walk in the woods?" he said.

Just then Mother Bear caught sight of the child, still asleep in the log.

"Wait a minute," she said. "There's a child in our log. I remember now. She came in last October when the snow was falling. She called me Mother."

"She looks like breakfast to me," said Father Bear.

"Don't be so unkind," scolded Mother Bear. "I'm going to wake her up."

So Father Bear went off on his own feeling grumpy, and Mother Bear gently woke the sleeping child.

"Good morning, poppet," she said, licking the child with her warm wet tongue. "Did you sleep well?"

"Yes thank you, Mother," said the child. "Once I found you I slept like a log."

"In a log," corrected Mother Bear gently. "You slept *in* a log. And now it is spring. My cubs have gone off into the wide world to seek their fortunes, and I suppose you'll be wanting to do the same."

"Will I?" asked the child.

"I expect so," said Mother Bear, with a sigh.

The child looked at herself. She had grown, but not as much as the young bears. She had found a mother. She had slept through the spring and through the bitter winter, safe on her mother's belly.

"If it's all the same to you, Mother," she said, "I will stay with you through the spring, and through the summer and the autumn too. I will sleep one more winter with you in the hollow log. After that, I may go off to seek my fortune. I'll see how I feel."

Mother Bear smiled a warm wide smile. "It's better than all the same to me, my child," she answered.

"Then I'll stay," said the child. And she did.

Wouldn't you?

Why Do Stars Come Out at Night?

Annalena McAfee and Anthony Lewis

Why do stars come out
at night?
Because the moon is scared
of the dark.

Why do we fall asleep?

Because our dreams must go out to play.

WHAT IS THE MOON?
Caroline Dunant and Liz Loveless

What is the moon?
It's a light in the sky that makes
the dark bright.

105

Does it shine every night?
Sometimes we can't see it
but the moon is still there.

But where is it, where?
It might go behind clouds,
maybe to sleep,
or to play
hide and seek.

Will it play with me?
We'll see, but now
it's time for your tea.
Why is the moon so high?
What's it doing up there?
At the top of the world,
like the top of a tree,
the moon hangs by a ribbon
that no one can see.

What colour is it?
Why doesn't it show?
And how do you know?
I was told it is black, a long time ago.

Can I fly up and see?
Not just now. It's time for your tea.

Is the moon very old?
Is it hot, is it cold?

The moon changes shape,
but it has always been there.
You would need a coat,
or something warm to wear.

What shapes do you mean?
Can you please show me?
I will, and then it's
time for your tea.
Now, hold up your hands
and we will try
to make shapes of the moon
changing in the sky.

Into the curve of the right,
fits the moon when it's new.

Make a circle with both
and the full moon's in view.

Then curve to the left,
to fit the moon when it's old.
And that is what I was always told.

Can you do that again?
Can I try?
Can I see how the moon fits together with my hands and me?
Just once more, then you must have your tea.

But there's still so much that I don't know.
Is the moon made of snow?
There are mountains and valleys and wide open spaces.

It looks too small to have so many places.

The moon is a world as big as ours but no people are there, it just lives with the stars.

That sounds very sad. I'll fly up and see
if the moon would like to play with me.
No, not right now, it's so far away,
to get there would take a year and a day.

But look at the sky, the moon is so near.
It seems that way, because the night is clear.

But Mum, can't you see, it's waving to me...
I'm going right now to the moon for my tea.

THE SWAN
Virginia Mayo

One day Mum and Rob and I went to the country.
We had a picnic. Mum said if we were lucky we might see
some ducks or geese. We were very lucky. We saw a *swan*.

He swam very close to me. "Hello," I said.
Mum told me that swans fall in love and stay together
all their lives. If they are parted, the one left behind is
so sad that it pines away and dies.

Then I noticed a fisherman and his little boy. Their line broke
and the fisherman threw it back in the water.
Mum was angry. She said the swans could get tangled in his line
and the lead weights could poison them. I thought perhaps the
man didn't know that he might hurt the swans, so I told him.
"Mind your own business!" he said.

Back at home I told Mum that I didn't understand how anyone could hurt animals.

I thought about my swan and how he had looked at me as if I was his friend.

That night I had a dream. Someone tapped at my window.

When I woke up, for a moment I didn't know where I was.
Then I remembered my dream.
Mum came in to get me dressed. "Look," she said. "A swan's
feather. It must have caught on your clothes."

Later that summer we went back to the river.
We took a picnic. Mum said if we were lucky we might see some
swans. We were *very* lucky. We saw a mum and a dad and six babies!
"Swans fall in love and stay together all their lives," I told Rob.
They swam up close to show me their babies... and they looked
right at me as if they knew I was their friend.

Acknowledgements

THE PUBLISHERS GRATEFULLY ACKNOWLEDGE PERMISSION TO REPRODUCE THE
FOLLOWING STORIES, WHICH ARE PUBLISHED IN LONGER, COMPLETE EDITIONS
UNDER THEIR OWN IMPRINTS:

Frog is Frightened, © 1994 by Max Velthuijs,
reprinted by permission of Lothrop, Lee & Shepard Books, and Andersen Press

From One Round Moon and a Star For Me by Ingrid Mennen, illustrated by Niki Daly.
Text copyright © 1994 by Ingrid Mennen. Illustrations copyright © 1994 by Niki Daly.
Reprinted by permission of Orchard Books, New York.

Rabbit Magic, published by The Bodley Head,
text © 1993 by Susie Jenkin-Pearce, illustrations © 1993 by Julia Malim

Timid Tim and the Cuggy Thief, published by The Bodley Head,
© 1993 by John Prater

Bedtime: Little Princess Board Books, copyright © 1995 by Tony Ross,
reprinted by permission of Harcourt Brace & Company, and Andersen Press

Burning the Tree, from *Stories by Firelight*, © 1993 by Shirley Hughes,
reprinted by permission of Lothrop, Lee & Shepard Books

Dad! I Can't Sleep, © 1994 by Michael Foreman,
reprinted by permission of Andersen Press

I Want to See the Moon, published by The Bodley Head,
text © 1984 by Louis Baum, illustrations © 1984 by Niki Daly

Someone Somewhere, published by The Bodley Head,
text © 1995 by Henrietta Branford, illustrations © 1995 by Lesley Harker

Why Do Stars Come Out at Night? (an extract), published by Julia MacRae Books,
text © 1997 by Annalena McAfee, illustrations © 1997 by Anthony Lewis

What is the Moon? published by The Bodley Head,
text © 1993 by Caroline Dunant, illustrations © 1993 by Liz Loveless

The Swan, published by The Bodley Head,
© 1993 by Virgina Mayo

Cuddle Up Tight

CONTENTS

WALKING ROUND THE GARDEN

John Prater

Walking round the garden, like a teddy bear,

One step, two steps, tickle you under there.

Walking down the hallway, up and up the stairs,

One step, two steps, what a clever bear!

Sitting in the bedroom,

What a sleepy ted,

All I need is a goodnight kiss,

Then tuck you into bed.

AN EVENING
AT ALFIE'S

Shirley Hughes

Oa cold, winter evening, Alfie and his little sister, Annie Rose,
were all ready for bed. Mum and Dad were all ready to go out,
and Mrs MacNally's Maureen was in the living-room. She had
come to look after Alfie and Annie Rose while Mum and Dad
went to a party.

Alfie and Maureen waved
good-bye to them from
the window.

Annie Rose was
already in her cot.
Soon she settled
down and went to sleep.

Alfie liked Maureen. She always read him a story when she came to baby-sit.

Tonight Alfie wanted the story about Noah and his Ark full of animals. Alfie liked to hear how the rain came drip, drip, drip, and then splash! splash! splash! and then rushing everywhere, until the whole world was covered with water.

When Maureen had finished the story it was time for Alfie to go to bed. She came upstairs to tuck him up.

They had to be very quiet and talk in whispers in case they woke up Annie Rose.

Maureen gave Alfie a good-night hug and went off downstairs, leaving the door a little bit open.

Alfie didn't feel sleepy. He lay in bed
looking at the patch of light on the ceiling.

For a long time all was quiet.
Then he heard a funny noise
outside on the landing.

Alfie sat up. The noise was
just outside his door. Drip,
drip, drip! Soon it got quicker.
It changed to drip-drip,
drip-drip, drip-drip! It was
getting louder too.

Alfie got out of bed and peeped round the door. There was a puddle on the floor. He looked up. Water was splashing into the puddle from the ceiling, drip-drip, drip-drip, drip-drip! It was raining inside the house!

Alfie went downstairs. Maureen was doing her homework in front of the television.

"It's raining on the landing," Alfie told her.

Alfie and Maureen went back upstairs. The puddle was getting bigger. The drip-drip, drip-drip, drip-drip had turned into a splash! splash! splash!

"Hmm, looks like a burst pipe," said Maureen. A plumber was one of the things she wanted to be when she left school.

"Better get a bucket," she said. So Alfie showed her where the bucket was kept, in the kitchen cupboard with the brushes and brooms.

But now the water was dripping down in another place.

Alfie and Maureen found two of Mum's big mixing bowls and put them underneath the drips.

Maureen got on the telephone to her Mum. The MacNallys lived just across the street.

Mrs MacNally was there
in a moment.
    "Oh dear, oh dear, it's
ruining your mother's
floor!" cried Mrs MacNally.
"Fetch some floor-cloths,
Maureen!"

Just then Annie Rose woke up and began to cry.
    "Shh, shh, there, there," said Mrs MacNally, bending over her cot.
But Annie Rose only looked at her and cried louder.

Mrs MacNally ran back out to the landing. She and Maureen tried to mop up the water. But now the drips were coming from lots of different places, splash, splash, splash!

"We ought to turn the water off from the main," said Maureen, "but I don't know how you do it. I think I'd better fetch Dad."

While she was gone Mrs MacNally mopped and mopped, and emptied brimming bowls, and in between mopping and emptying she ran to try to comfort Annie Rose. But Annie Rose went on crying and crying. The drips on the landing came faster and faster.

Now there were a lot of puddles on the floor. Alfie paddled in them for a while. It was quite fun but the water was very cold. He thought that soon perhaps the whole street would be covered with water and they would all have to float away in a boat, like Noah's Ark.

Soon Maureen came running upstairs with Mr MacNally close behind her, wearing his bedroom slippers.

"What's all this, then?" said Mr MacNally, looking at all the water pouring down.

He put his head round the bedroom door. He and Annie Rose were old friends.

"Dear, dear, what's all this?" he said in a very kind voice.

Then he went downstairs and found a large sort of tap under the stairs and turned it off, just like that.

"So *that's* where it was," said Maureen.

Then the water stopped pouring down through the ceiling, splash! splash! splash! and became a

      drip-drip, drip-drip,
      drip-drip, and then
   a drip... drip.... drip..... drip...... and then
    it stopped altogether.

     "Oh, thank goodness for that!" said Mrs MacNally.

     "I'll know how to do it next time," said Maureen.

     But Annie Rose was still crying.

Alfie went into the bedroom
to see if he could cheer her up.
Tears were rolling down her
cheeks and soaking into her
blanket.

"Don't cry, Annie Rose," said Alfie. And he put
his hand through the bars of her cot and patted her very gently,
as he had seen Mum do sometimes.

Annie Rose still wore nappies at night.

"Annie Rose is wet," Alfie told everyone. "And her bed's wet too.
I expect that's why she's crying."

"Why, so she is, poor little mite!" said Mrs MacNally.

When Annie Rose was all dry and comfortable again, Mrs MacNally put her on the living-room sofa with Alfie and tucked a quilt round them. Then she gave them both a biscuit.

Annie Rose was quite cheerful now. She got very friendly with Mr MacNally and he let her play a game with him, taking off his glasses and putting them on again.

Then she sucked her thumb and leaned up against Alfie, and Alfie leaned up against her. When Mum and Dad came home, they were both fast asleep.

Next morning Mum told Alfie not to turn on the taps until the plumber had been to mend the burst pipe.

Alfie didn't mind not having a wash. He'd had enough water the evening before to last for a long time.

TOO MANY TEDDIES

Gus Clarke

"Mum," said Frank. "There are just too many teddies."
"Nonsense," said Mum. "You can never have too many teddies."

But Frank did.

It started the day he was born. "A boy needs a bear," said Uncle Jim. And that was the first...

of many.

He'd get them for birthdays and for Christmas...

for all sorts of special occasions...

and sometimes for no particular reason at all.

By the time he was four there was more than a bed full. There were teddies everywhere.

And even the teddies had teddies.

At bedtime his dad would tuck them all in and together they would say goodnight to them. One by one.

It seemed to Frank that if he got many more teddies, by the time they'd said goodnight to them all it would be time to get up!

It was then that Frank knew he'd really got a problem. But the more he thought about it, the more he could see that the problem was not the teddies...

the problem was Dad...
and Mum...

...and all the aunties and uncles, the grandmas and grandpas, the cousins, the friends and the neighbours that kept on giving him all these teddies.

He knew that they all liked teddies and he knew that they all liked choosing the teddies. They'd told him.

They'd spend ages choosing the cuddliest one, or the cutest one, the furriest or the funniest one, the one with the special smile...

or even just the one with the squeakiest tummy.

In fact, just the sort of teddy that they would like for themselves. But, of course, being so grown up they thought they couldn't really buy it for themselves.
So they bought it for Frank.
At least they could have a little cuddle before they gave it to him.

And that was when he had his idea. Perhaps, thought Frank, if they all had a teddy of their own to cuddle, they wouldn't need to buy quite so many for him.

"Grandma," said Frank. "Would you like to look after my teddy for a little while? I've got plenty more."
And, of course, Grandma was only too pleased.

And so was Aunty Vicky...

and Uncle Roger...

and Cousin Percy...

and the man next door but one.
And everyone else.

Of course, Frank kept one or two for himself – his favourites, and one or two more to keep them company.

And that was that.
They all lived happily ever after. Until one day...

"A boy needs a dog," said Uncle Jim.   And that...

...was the first of many.

NEARLY BUT NOT QUITE

Paul Rogers and John Prater

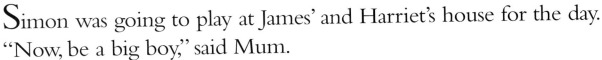

Simon was going to play at James' and Harriet's house for the day.
"Now, be a big boy," said Mum.
But Simon didn't feel very big.
And he didn't wave goodbye
when she went, either.
He stood at the bottom of
the garden steps and looked
around him at the big house,
the big lawn and the great
big trees.

"Come on," said James,
"let's play Robin Hood."
"This can be the camp,"
said Harriet. "Can you
climb up?"

"Nearly," said Simon...

"...but not quite."

"We'll get the supper ready.
You keep a look out,"
said James.
"Can you see over the top?"
said Harriet.

"Nearly," said Simon...

"...but not quite."

"Quick!" said James,
"the sheriff's men
are coming! We're
under attack!"

"Can you fire
a bow and
arrow?"
said Harriet.

"Nearly,"
said Simon...

"...but not quite."

"Look! They're giving themselves up!" said James. "They're waving a white flag!"
"Where?" said Simon. "I can't see it."

"Give me your t-shirt," said Harriet. "But you mustn't tell."
"Big boys don't tell," said James.

"Watch out! It's a trap!"
said James.
"We'll have to escape by
the secret passage. There's
no time to lose."
"Wait for me!" said Simon.

"Where have you
been?" said James.
"Did you get caught?"
"Nearly," said Simon...

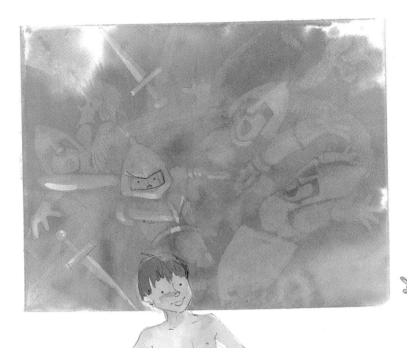

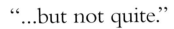

"...but not quite."

"They're still behind us!" said Harriet.
"There's only one thing for it! We must
take the horses."
"Here's yours," said James. "Do you
know how to ride?"

"Nearly," said Simon...

"...but not quite."

"They're following our tracks," said James. "Leave the horses here. We'll cross the river."

"Can you step over?" said Harriet.

"Nearly," said Simon...

"... but not quite."

"James? Harriet?" called a voice.
"Simon, your mum's here!"
James and Harriet looked at Simon.

Then they looked at each
other. "I want Mummy,"
said Simon.

"What do you want your mum for?" said James.
"I thought you were a big boy," said Harriet.

"Nearly,"
said Simon...

"...but not quite!"

Hallo! How Are You?

Shigeo Watanabe and Yasuo Ohtomo

"Hallo, flowers.
How are you?"

"Hallo, sparrows.
How are you?"

"Hallo, cat.
How are you?"

"Hallo, dog.
How are you?"

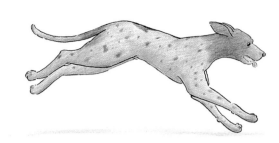

"Hallo, Mr Milkman.
How are you?"

"Hallo, Mr Paperman.
How are you?"

"Hallo, Mr Postman.
How are you?"

"Hallo, Mama.
How are you?"

"What a funny little bear you are."

"Wait. Wait!"

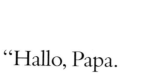

"Hallo, Papa.
How are you?"

"Hallo, Little Bear.
I'm very well,
thank you.
How are you?"

ANYONE SEEN HARRY LATELY?

Hiawyn Oram and Tony Ross

Whenever Harry did not like the way things looked, he disappeared...

re-appearing as some other Harry, for Harrysaurs are not required to tidy rooms or hang up clothes,

Harrylions are never
left with babysitters
half the night,

and Harryfish
are free to swim
and never told
to wash their ears
because they
have none.

49

So while others
fought their battles
face to face Harry
sailed behind some
great disguises and
got away unscratched.

He thought,
"Well, this is
fun and this is
peaceful," and
started doing it
all the time and
couldn't stop
himself

and then
forgot himself.

His mother was
the first to notice.
"Anyone seen
Harry lately?
I went to tuck
him up in bed
and found a
Harrygator."

His father went next door
to ask, "Anyone seen Harry
lately?"
The neighbours scratched
their heads and hummed,
"A Harrybat was here
last night - but Harry -
not for ages."

His friends came round
and rang the bell.

His mother, pale and cross, peered out, "Any of you seen
Harry lately?"
A Harrytank zoomed down the stairs and through the door
and up the street.
His friends said, "Nice - but that's not him.
We've not seen Harry lately."

52

He sat unfed.
(No one feeds strange
Harrystricters.)

He lay unkissed
(no one kisses
Harrybeetles) and
wondered where
he'd lost himself
along the road to
peace and quiet.

"I'd better have a search," he said
and called up all the characters
he'd used to wriggle out of things

and made them line up round the room
and stand there, marking time, all night.

But though he studied
carefully he couldn't
see himself at all.
Or wait a minute...
what was that...

the sudden
narrowing of eyes...
the rudest little
tongue pulled out.
"Ah ha," he said,
"this looks like me..."
and urged his
characters to worse.

"Go on. Let's see. Get more like me.
Refuse to do what you are told,
to be the things you're
made to be."

Well, taking Harry at his word
and taking everything they'd need
those Harrycharacters made off
to find their own identity.

Still, good does
come of bad, because
a Harry stripped of all disguises
quickly re-materialises.

"Yoo hoo," he yelled
and ran into his
parents' room.
"Great news! Wake up!
I'm back! It's me!"
His parents rolled and
turned and stared.

"Who? Oh you!
Have you tidied up
your room?"
"Not yet," groaned
Harry, "maybe later.
Besides it wasn't me
who messed it.
I think it was that
Harrygator."

58

"It really is our
Harry back," his
parents sighed
and let him in
and held him
tight in case he
disappeared again

but Harry said,
"No chance
of that. Well,
not tonight
at any rate!"

IS THAT WHAT FRIENDS DO?

Marjorie Newman and Peter Bowman

Elephant sat gloomily on the river bank.
  Monkey came dancing along.
  "Hello, Elephant!" cried
Monkey. "All alone?"
  "Yes," sighed Elephant.
  "So am I!" said
Monkey. "Let's
be friends!"

  "I've never had a friend before," said Elephant.
  "I have. Lots!" cried Monkey.
"Why don't you come
and stay with me?"

"Is that what friends do?"
asked Elephant.

"Of course!" cried Monkey.

Monkey's doorway was too small for Elephant.

"Ow!" cried Elephant.

"Eee!" cried Elephant.

"Ah!" cried Elephant.

"I nearly got stuck."

"You are funny," cried Monkey, doubling up laughing, and not trying to help Elephant, *at all*.

Monkey switched on the radio.

The music was very loud.

"Let's dance!" cried Monkey.

"Is that what friends do?" asked Elephant.

"Of course!" cried Monkey. "Come on."

"Ow!" cried Elephant.
  "Eee!" cried Elephant.
  "Ah!" cried Elephant.
"I can't dance."

"You are funny," cried Monkey, spinning round on one leg, and
not trying to help Elephant, *at all*.

"We'll have scrambled eggs
on toast for supper,"
said Monkey.

"I don't like
scrambled eggs
on toast," said
Elephant.

"I do!" cried Monkey. "I'll let you be cook
and we'll eat supper together."

"Is that what friends do?" asked Elephant.

"Of course!" cried Monkey.

"Ah!" cried Elephant.

"Eee!" cried
Elephant.

"Ow!" cried
Elephant. "I
can't cook."

"You are funny!" laughed Monkey, sitting up at the table, and not
trying to help Elephant, *at all*.

"Bedtime," announced Monkey. "Stay
the night and you can sleep in my chair."

"Is that what friends do?" asked Elephant,
trying to make himself comfortable.
    "Of course," yawned
Monkey.

"Ow!"
cried Elephant.
    "Eee!" cried Elephant.
    "Ah!" cried Elephant. "I'm falling off."

Monkey didn't even stir.
He slept very well.
He snored very loudly.

Elephant didn't sleep one wink. Not even with
cotton wool stuffed into his ears.

Next morning, Monkey woke up early.

"Come on, Elephant," he cried. "Let's go climbing."

"I don't like climbing, especially before breakfast," said Elephant.

"I do," cried Monkey. "We can climb together."

"Is that what friends do?" asked Elephant.

"Of course!" cried Monkey, putting on his jacket.

Elephant shivered outside the door.

"Hurry up, Elephant!" called Monkey. "We can climb this tree."

"Is that what friends do?" asked Elephant.

"Of course!" cried Monkey, already shinning high into the branches.

Elephant started to climb.
Crack went the branch.
Crash went Elephant.
"Ahhhhhhhhhhh!" cried Elephant.

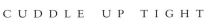

"Eee!" cried Elephant.

"Ow!" cried Elephant.

"I can't climb."

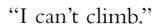

Monkey slid down the tree.
"Ah," said Monkey.
"Eee," said Monkey.
"Oh dear," said Monkey,
looking into a big
hole, and not
being able to see
Elephant, *at all*.

Monkey was all alone.

71

Further along the bank, Elephant sat gloomily. All alone.
Monkey came walking by.
"Oh, there you are,
Elephant," cried
Monkey.

"Go away!"
growled Elephant.

Monkey was very quiet.
"Elephant," he said, "you
know I said I'd had lots
of friends?"

"Yes,"
sighed
Elephant.

"Well," said Monkey, "none of them stayed friends for long."
Elephant was quiet. Monkey was quiet. They were thinking.

72

"Elephant," said Monkey, after a while, "perhaps I got it all wrong."

"Oh?" said Elephant.

"Elephant," said Monkey. "Perhaps friends are kind to each other and share things."

"Oh!" said Elephant.

"Elephant," said Monkey. "Shall we try again?"

"Is that what friends do?" asked Elephant.

"Of course!" cried Monkey.

And they gave each other a great, big hug.

Mr Bill and Clarence

Kay Gallwey

Mr Bill is a kitten with a smart ginger moustache and long whiskers.
His fur is ginger and white.
He has big green eyes and because he is a Manx kitten, he has only a short stumpy tail.
On the night Mr Bill arrived he was tucked into a box with teddy and a cosy cover.

But next morning, Mr Bill wasn't with teddy in the box, or on the chair, or on the sofa, he was with Clarence in his big basket.

Clarence is a big Collie dog, with a long golden coat, big white ruff, soft dark ears and big brown eyes.

Mr Bill loves him.

Mr Bill and Clarence have breakfast together.

Mr Bill tries a bit of Clarence's lunch. Clarence doesn't mind a bit. They share a juicy bone for tea.

75

Mr Bill and Clarence
love to play together.

They play jumping the sofa.

They play hide and seek.

Mr Bill loves to jump out
and surprise Clarence.

76

Mr Bill hasn't got
a tail to play with,
so he borrows
Clarence's.

Mr Bill grows and grows.

But he still borrows
Clarence's tail.

Clarence wants to
borrow Mr Bill's
cat door, but he
is too big.

Every night, Mr Bill
washes himself,

then he washes
Clarence.

Then they curl
up together in
their big basket,
and go to sleep.
It's a bit of a
squash, but they
don't mind a bit.

RUBY
Maggie Glen

Ruby felt different from other bears - sort of special.

Mrs Harris had been day-dreaming when she made Ruby. She didn't notice that she'd used the spotted material that was meant for the toy leopards. She didn't watch carefully when she sewed on the nose.

Ruby wasn't surprised when she was chosen from the other bears, but she didn't like being picked up by her ear.

"OUCH, GET OFF!" she growled.

Ruby's paw was stamped with an 'S' and she was thrown into the air.

"YIPEE-E-E-E! 'S' IS FOR SPECIAL," yelled Ruby.

Ruby flew across the factory and landed in a box full of bears.

"Hello," she said. "My name's Ruby and I'm special - see."

She held up her paw.

"No silly," laughed a big bear. "'S' is for second - second best."

"We're mistakes," said the bear with rabbit ears. "When the box is full, we'll be thrown out."

Ruby's fur stood on end; she was horrified.

More bears joined them in the box.

   At last the machines stopped.

   They listened to the workers as they
chatted and hurried to catch the bus home.

   They heard the key turn in the lock.

   Then everything was quiet.

   One by one the bears fell asleep.

   All except Ruby – Ruby was thinking.

   The only sound was the sound of the
big bear snoring.

Hours passed. Suddenly Ruby shouted, "That's it!"

"What's it?" gasped the rabbit-eared bear
who woke up with a fright.

"Zzzzzzzzzzzzzzzz-w-w-what's
going on?" groaned the big bear,
rubbing his sleepy eyes.

"That's *it*," said Ruby again. "We'll escape."

"ESCAPE!" they all shouted.
And they jumped out of the box.

"Let's go!" said Ruby.

They looked for a way out.
   They rattled the windows.
   They pushed at the doors.
   "There *is* no way out,"
cried a little bear.
"We're trapped."

"This way," shouted Ruby, rushing into the cloakroom.

84

They found a
broken air vent.
It was a very
tight squeeze.

They pushed and they pulled, they wiggled and they waggled, until
they were all in the yard outside.

They ran silently, swiftly, through the night and into the day.
Some ran to the country, some to the town.

Some squeezed
through letterboxes.

Some slipped through open windows.

Some hid in toy cupboards. Some crept into bed with lonely children.
But Ruby climbed into the window of the very best toy shop in town.

The other toys stared at Ruby.

"What's the 'S' for?" squealed the pigs.

"Special," said Ruby, proudly.

All the toys shrieked with laughter.

"Scruffy," said the smart-looking penguin.

"Soppy," said the chimpanzee.

"Stupid," giggled the mice.

"Very strange for a bear," they all agreed.

"Don't come next to me," said a prim doll.

"Wouldn't want to," said Ruby.

"Stand at the back," shouted the other toys.

They poked, they pulled, they prodded and they pinched. Ruby pushed back as hard as she could, but there were too many of them.

So Ruby spent all day at the back of the shelf.

Then, just before closing time, a small girl came into the shop with her grandfather.

They searched and searched for something – something different, something special.

"That's the one," said the little girl.

"Yes, Susie," said Grandfather, "that one looks very special."

Ruby looked around her. "Can they see me?"

"IT'S ME! They're pointing at me. WHOOPEE-E-E-E!"

"We'll have that one, please," said Grandfather.

The shopkeeper put Ruby on the counter.

She looked at the 'S' on Ruby's paw.

"I'm sorry, sir," she said, "this one is a second. I'll fetch another."

"No thank you, that one is just perfect," said Grandfather. "It has character."

Character, thought Ruby, that sounds good.

"Shall I wrap it for you?" the shopkeeper asked.

"Not likely," growled Ruby. "Who wants to be shoved in a paper bag?"

"No thank you," said Susie. "I'll have her just as she is."

They all went out of the shop and down the street.

When they came to a yellow door they stopped.

"We're home, Spotty," said Susie.

"SPOTTY, WHAT A CHEEK!" muttered Ruby.

"It's got a growl," said Susie, and she and her grandfather laughed.

Susie took off her coat and scarf and sat Ruby on her lap.

Susie stared at Ruby and Ruby stared back.

Suddenly, Ruby saw a little silver 'S' hanging on a chain round Susie's neck.

Hooray! thought Ruby.

One of us – a special.

ALL THE WAY TO THE STARS

Annalena McAfee and Anthony Lewis

I've had a lot of birthdays,
I even go to school.
I ride my bike all
on my own,

and like to help around
the house.

But every day
my mummy says,
"Don't do that!
That's for big boys!"

When I'm big...

I'll climb to the top of the tower and stay up
all night to hear the owls hoot.

I'll eat all the sweets
in the sweetshop

and ride a really huge bike.

When I'm a big boy
I'll teach my teacher,
and send my
mummy to bed
early for
being naughty.

94

I'll drive a big
red bus to
the seaside,

go on
every ride
at the funfair,
and no-one will
ever say, "Don't
do that! That's
for big boys!"

I'll visit the zoo and join the monkeys for tea.
I'll have a pet pig and take him for walks in the woods.

95

When I'm a big boy,
I'll sail a ship to the top
and bottom of the world
to see the koalas in Australia,

the tigers in India,

the bears in Alaska, and the penguins in Antarctica.

I'll find heaps of buried treasure
when I'm a big boy,
and fight off silly pirates,

and keep a parrot
that sings rude songs.

When I'm a big boy
I'll fly a plane all the
way to the stars. And
make sandcastles on
the moon.

But I'll still come home to play with my toys

and see my mummy.

NANA'S GARDEN

Sophy Williams

One day in early autumn, Thomas was going out to play.

"You come too, Nana," he said.

"Me?" said Nana. "I'm too old to play."

"I wish you weren't," said Thomas.

The sun cast shadows in Nana's garden. Thomas kicked up the leaves, still wet from the morning's rain. A branch cracked, an apple fell.

"Who's there?" said Thomas. The wind in the trees murmured, *"It's only me. An echo, a whisper, a heartbeat."*

The air grew cold in Nana's garden. Thomas turned and looked around. The long grass was flattened as if someone had been walking there. A trail of footsteps seemed to run in and out of the trees. Thomas followed them, all round the orchard and across the lawn to Nana's shed.

Thomas had never been inside, but now he thought perhaps there was something precious hidden there.

As he reached up to open the door, he thought he saw someone watching him.

"Who's there?" he said.

The wind whistled under the door. *"Inside,"* it said. *"Inside."*

A pale light shone through the little window, and lit up the muddle inside. Thomas began to search. Through the ancient chest of drawers, behind an old mirror, inside a box of rusty tools.

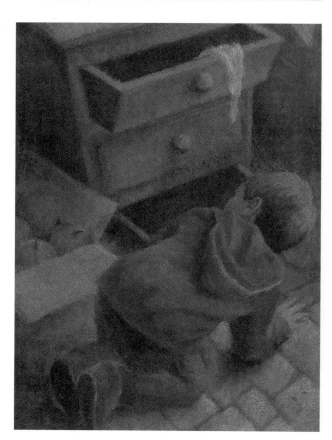

Then at the back of the shed Thomas found a tall cupboard. He opened the door. Dust flew up in a cloud. Spiders and mice scuttled. From a dark corner, a worn, friendly face looked out at him.

Very gently, very carefully, Thomas lifted out the treasure.

At the window, the small fingers of another child gripped the sill. There was a shimmer of blue, a wisp of hair, a bright eye watching.

"*There, there,*" sang the other child. "*He's been waiting, all these long years.*"

Thomas hugged the treasure and took it outside. As he sat on the damp grass he felt a tap on his shoulder.

"*Hello.*"

"Hello," said Thomas. "Who are you? This is Nana's garden."

"*It's my garden too,*" said the other child. "*I've come for Joshua.*"

"But I found him," said Thomas.

"*I know,*" she said. "*But he's mine.*"

The wind was very still. Thomas looked at the little girl.

"Let's play," he said.

They played with Joshua.

They played I-spy and giant's footsteps. They played statues and hide-and-seek. The sun came out. They raced in and out the trees - all around the orchard and up the steps.

"Come on," said the other child. "I'll show you the secret places."

They ran through Nana's garden to the wild part where Thomas had never been before. Brambles caught at their clothes, leaves crunched under their feet.

"Look Thomas," said the other child. *"This is where Josie and Tsar are buried. Josie was a big sad labrador. Tsar was a snappy little terrier. He pined for days when Josie died. He didn't last long after."*

"And see that rose over there," said the child. *"I planted it because my name is Rose."*

"Nana's name is Rose too," said Thomas.

The light began to fade in Nana's garden.

"*I'm tired now,*" said Rose. "*I've got to go.*"

"Don't go," said Thomas. "Stay with me."

"*I am with you,*" she said. "*I'm always with you.*"

"Please don't go," said Thomas again.

110

But Rose was already through the gate. Thomas ran after her. "Here, take Joshua," he said. "He's yours."

Then the light was gone in Nana's garden. There was no one there. Just an echo, a shadow, a heartbeat.

Thomas ran back inside and hugged his grandmother fiercely.

"I love you, Nana," he said.

FROG IN LOVE
Max Velthuijs

Frog was sitting on the river bank.
He felt funny.
He didn't know if he was happy or sad.
He had been walking about in a dream all week.
What could be wrong with him?

Then he met Piglet.

"Hello, Frog," said Piglet. "You don't look
very well. What's the matter with you?"

"I don't know," said Frog. "I feel like
laughing and crying at the same time.
And there's something going thump-thump
inside me, here."

"Maybe you've caught a cold," said Piglet.
"You'd better go home to bed."

Frog went on his way. He was worried.

Then he passed
Hare's house.
"Hare," he said,
"I don't feel well."
"Come along in and
sit down," said Hare,
kindly.
"Now then," said
Hare, "what's the
matter with you?"
"Sometimes I go hot,
and sometimes I go
cold," said Frog, "and

there's something going thump-thump inside me, here."
And he put his hand on his chest.
Hare thought hard, just like a real doctor.
"I see," he said. "It's your heart. Mine goes thump-thump too."

"But mine sometimes
thumps faster than usual,"
said Frog. "It goes one-two,
one-two, one-two."
Hare took a big book down
from his bookshelf and
turned the pages.
"Aha!" he said. "Listen to
this. Heartbeat, speeded up,
hot and cold turns...
it means you're in love!"
"In love?" said Frog, surprised. "Wow, I'm in love!"

And he was so pleased that
he did a tremendous jump
right out of the door and
up in the air.

Piglet was quite
scared when Frog
suddenly came
falling from the sky.
"You seem to be
better," said Piglet.
"I am! I feel just
fine," said Frog.
"I'm in love!"
"Well, that's good
news. Who are
you in love with?"
asked Piglet.

Frog hadn't stopped to think about that.
"I know!" he said. "I'm in love with the pretty, nice, lovely white duck!"
"You can't be," said Piglet. "A frog can't be in love with a duck.
You're green and she's white."

But Frog didn't let
that bother him.
He couldn't write,
but he could do
beautiful paintings.
Back at home he
painted a lovely
picture, with red
and blue in it and
lots of green, his
favourite colour.

In the evening, when it was dark, he went out with his picture and pushed it under the door of Duck's house. His heart was beating hard with excitement.

Duck was very surprised when she found the picture. "Who can have sent me this beautiful picture?" she cried, and she hung it on the wall.

Next day Frog picked a beautiful bunch of flowers. He was going to give them to Duck. But when he reached her door, he felt too shy to face her. He put the flowers down on the doorstep and ran away as fast as he could go.

And so it went on, day after day. Frog just couldn't pluck up the courage to speak. Duck was very pleased with all her lovely presents. But who could be sending them?

Poor Frog! He didn't enjoy his food any more, and he couldn't sleep at night. Things went on like this for weeks. How could he show Duck he loved her?

"I must do something nobody else can do," he decided. "I must break the world high jump record! Dear Duck will be very surprised, and then she'll love me back."

Frog started training at once. He practised the high jump for days on end. He jumped higher and higher, right up to the clouds. No frog in the world had ever jumped so high before.

"What can be the matter with Frog?" asked Duck, worried. "Jumping like that is dangerous. He'll do himself an injury." She was right.

At thirteen minutes past two on Friday afternoon, things went wrong. Frog was doing the highest jump in history when he lost his balance and fell to the ground.

Duck, who happened to be passing at the time, came hurrying up to help him. Frog could hardly walk. Supporting him carefully, she took him home with her. She nursed him with tender loving care.

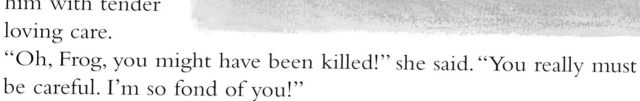

"Oh, Frog, you might have been killed!" she said. "You really must be careful. I'm so fond of you!"

And then, at last, Frog plucked up his courage. "I'm very fond of you too, dear Duck," he stammered. His heart was going thump-thump faster than ever, and his face turned deep green.

Ever since then, they have loved each other dearly.
A frog and a duck...
Green and white.
Love knows no boundaries.

Acknowledgements

THE PUBLISHERS GRATEFULLY ACKNOWLEDGE PERMISSION TO REPRODUCE THE
FOLLOWING STORIES, WHICH ARE PUBLISHED IN LONGER, COMPLETE EDITIONS
BY ANDERSEN PRESS:

Too Many Teddies © Gus Clarke 1995

Anyone Seen Harry Lately? Text © Hiawyn Oram 1988, Illustrations © Tony Ross 1988

Frog in Love © Max Velthuijs 1989

THE PUBLISHERS GRATEFULLY ACKNOWLEDGE AUTHORS AND ILLUSTRATORS
OF BOOKS PUBLISHED UNDER THEIR OWN IMPRINTS AS FOLLOWS:

Walking Round the Garden, published by The Bodley Head,
© John Prater 1998
Thanks also to Barron's Educational, New York

An Evening at Alfie's, published by The Bodley Head,
© Shirley Hughes 1984

Nearly But Not Quite, published by The Bodley Head,
Text © Paul Rogers 1997, Illustrations © John Prater 1997

Hallo! How Are You?, published by The Bodley Head,
Text © Shigeo Watanabe 1979, English text © The Bodley Head 1980,
Illustrations © Yasuo Ohtomo 1979
Thanks also to Fukuinkan Shoten, Japan

Is That What Friends Do?, published by Hutchinson Children's Books,
Text © Marjorie Newman 1998, Illustrations © Peter Bowman 1998

Mr Bill and Clarence, published by The Bodley Head,
© Kay Gallwey 1990

Ruby, published by Hutchinson Children's Books,
© Maggie Glen 1990

All the Way to the Stars, published by Julia MacRae Books,
Text © Annalena McAfee 1995, Illustrations © Anthony Lewis 1995

Nana's Garden, published by Hutchinson Children's Books,
© Sophy Williams 1993
Thanks also to Viking, US

Sweet Dreams

 # CONTENTS

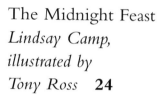

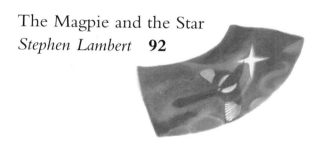

MY BLANKET IS BLUE

Hilda Offen

(WHISPER)   *My* blanket is soft,
My blanket is blue.

When Mum says, "Sleep tight",
Do you know what I do?

I say to my friends,
"Are you ready to go?
Let's fly to the North
And play in the snow!"

With the moon to our left
And the stars to our right,
We fly through the sky –
We fly through the night!

My blanket is cuddly –

It's warmer than toast.

I can scare off the bears.
"Shoo, Bears! I'm a ghost!"

(WHISPER) *My blanket is soft,*
My blanket is blue.

12

"Let's go," says the cat.
"It's too cold for me!"

So we fly to the South
And swim in the sea.

I can lie in my hammock
Or sit in the shade.

I can play Bouncing Bears
And drink lemonade.

(WHISPER) *My blanket is soft,*
My blanket is blue.

I can stand on my head,

Ask a tiger to tea,

Tuck him up if he's ill.

So – Three Cheers for me!

We can ride on an elephant
Down to the bay

Where my boat will be waiting
To take us away.

We sail on the sea,
We sail through the night –

All the way to my room
Where Mum says, "Sleep tight!"

My friends sigh and yawn;
They snuggle down, too.

(WHISPER)   *My blanket is soft,*
             My blanket is blue.

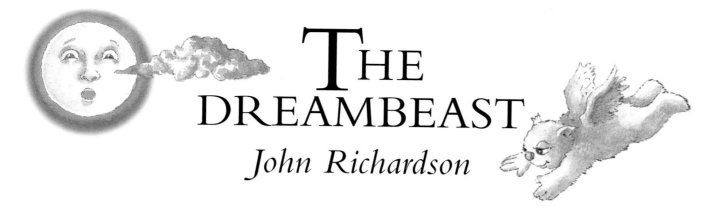

THE DREAMBEAST

John Richardson

Deep in a dark distant forest lives the Dreambeast. He sleeps in the morning, he plays snakes and ladders in the afternoon and he brings the children their dreams at night.

One day the Dreambeast couldn't sleep. He lost every game of snakes and ladders. "Bother!" he said, and grew very grumpy and cross.

"Bother!" he grumbled as he set off on his night rounds. "Bother," he called to the moon as he flew past.

That night he couldn't find any good dreams to put in little Tom's head.

First Tom dreamt that there was nothing to eat but cabbages...
and cabbages...
and more cabbages.

Then he dreamt that everyone had forgotten him at Christmas.

Next he dreamt a terrible blizzard blew his favourite teddy away!

Tom jumped up in bed and cried, "MUM!"

Mum came and kissed him better. She shook her fist at the night crying, "Naughty Dreambeast! You should be ashamed."

The Dreambeast was sorry for what he had done. He sat in his den feeling tired and sad, but *still* he couldn't sleep.

That night he went to Tom again.

Tom dreamt of a sad Dreambeast who couldn't sleep. In his dream he captured the beast and taught him his own bedtime secrets.

He shared his teddy and his mug of milk and his enormous comfy quilt. Then he read the Dreambeast a story.

Back in his den, the Dreambeast made a quilt of wool. He found his old teddy and boiled up a mug of milk with a little honey...

and slept and slept and slept and slept.

When he woke up he danced for joy.

That night Tom dreamt
of merry-go-rounds;
of candy sticks
and lollipops.

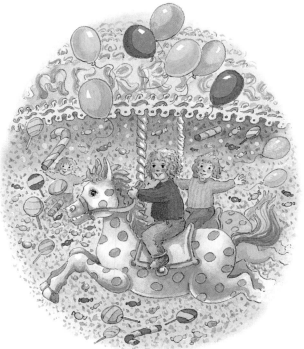

He dreamt that he flew through
clouds of blue, and over trees
with peaches and pears.

He dreamt of a
giant birthday cake
and of a party with
everyone there.

And he dreamt of that old Dreambeast
as he waved him a fond farewell.

THE MIDNIGHT FEAST

Lindsay Camp and Tony Ross

At bathtime, Alice whispered something to Freddie.

"Night night, love," said Mum, stretching to kiss Alice in the top bunk. "Night night, poppet," she said, bending to kiss Freddie in the bottom bunk.

As soon as Mum was gone, Alice climbed out of bed.

Come on, we've got to get ready.

She pulled the quilt off Freddie's bed and spread it on the floor. "That's for the beautiful princess to sit on."

What beautiful princess?

We must hurry, she'll be arriving soon.

Alice took a plastic bag from under the bunks and looked inside.
"We need some more food. I don't think beautiful princesses
like salt and vinegar crisps."

Freddie crept downstairs...

...and went to look for pomegranates and lobsters.
Mum was tidying the playroom and he didn't think she heard him.
When Freddie got back, Alice was sitting on his quilt.
She took the lobsters and pomegranates from him.

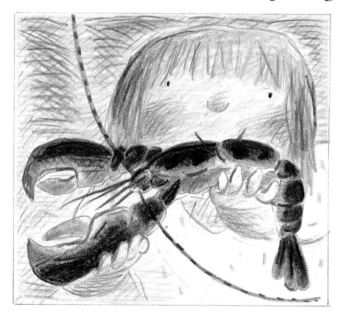 

Alice wriggled a bit on Freddie's quilt. "I don't think beautiful
princesses like sitting on ordinary quilts. We need a soft golden
cushion. Go and find one."

Freddie crept
downstairs...

...and went to
hunt for a soft
golden cushion.

A floorboard creaked, but Mum was in the kitchen now
and she was humming to herself quite loudly.

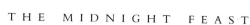

When he got back, Alice was just making sure that one of the pomegranates was sweet enough.

Alice licked juice off her chin, and Freddie gave her the soft golden cushion.

Freddie hurried
downstairs, and
nearly tripped
over Beelzebub.
But Mum had
turned on the TV...

...so she didn't hear.

When Freddie got back, Alice was sitting on the soft golden
cushion, licking one of the lobsters.
The last one.

Alice took the enchanted musical box from him.

Is she still
not here?

No...

...but it's very
nearly midnight.

So, just sit down quietly,

and we'll wait for the
beautiful princess to arrive.

Freddie sat down next to Alice...

...and waited.

A few minutes passed.

Shall I go and look for some more pomegranates and lobsters before the beautiful princess comes?

It's all right. I don't think she'll be very hungry. And if she is, I suppose she could eat the salt and vinegar crisps.

Freddie waited some more.

"When will she come?" he yawned. "It must be midnight now."

But Alice didn't answer.

A little later, the door opened, and someone came in. She covered Alice with a quilt, and kissed her. She lifted Freddie gently into bed and covered him too. Then she kissed him. Freddie opened his eyes for a moment.

"I knew you'd come," he whispered, "my sister said so." And then Freddie closed his eyes and went back to sleep.

And dreamed all night of a beautiful princess
holding him in her arms.

COUNTING COWS

Dyan Sheldon and Wendy Smith

Dara can't sleep.

"When I can't sleep, I count sheep," says Dara's father.

"I don't want to count sheep," says Dara.

Her father looks at her. "Why not?" he asks.

"Because I don't like sheep," says Dara. "I like cows."

"Count cows then," says Dara's father.

Dara frowns. "But what colour are the cows?"

"Shut your eyes," says Dara's father. "Ready now?" Dara's father leans back in his chair. "Imagine it's a sunny day. A herd of brown cows is standing in a large green field. There's a fence around the field. The cows start to move towards the fence. One by one they begin to jump. Count them slowly, Dara. One…two…three…"

"What's wrong?" asks her father. "Aren't the brown cows moving?"

"Oh, the brown cows are moving all right," says Dara. "But the black-and-white cow is just lying on her side, gazing up at the sky."

"She's doing what?" asks Dara's father.

"I think she must be counting the clouds in the sky," says Dara.

"Let's begin again, shall we?" Dara's father makes himself comfortable. "Close your eyes," he says. "Tell me what you see."

Dara tells him. "I see a sunny day. I see a big green field. There's a fence around the field. I see a herd of cows. All of the cows are brown except the one that's black and white."

"And is the black-and-white cow moving?"

"Oh, yes," says Dara. "She's moving."

"Well that's good," says Dara's father.

"She's dancing around the field."

"Dancing around the field?"

Dara smiles. "Yes," she says. "I think it must be because the butterflies are tickling her so much."

"Now look here," says Dara's father sternly. "It's getting late. No more of this gazing at the clouds nonsense. No more being tickled by butterflies. Let's get ALL the cows over to the fence."

"I'll try," says Dara. She closes her eyes.

"What's happening?" asks her father.

"The cows are going to the fence."

"Even the black-and-white cow?" asks her father.

"Oh, yes," says Dara. "Of course she is. That's where the best flowers are."

Dara's father opens one eye. "What flowers?"

"The flowers that my cow is picking," says Dara.

"Picking?" repeats Dara's father. "Cows can't pick flowers."

"My cow can," says Dara. "She's picking them to put on her hat."

"Shall we start again?" Dara's father leans back in his chair and makes himself very very comfortable. "Shut your eyes."

Dara's eyes shut tight.

"Right," says Dara's father. "Your cow looks up and she sees the cows all running across the field. Is she looking up, Dara?"

"She's looking up."

"But not at the clouds," says Dara's father. "Or the butterflies. She stops picking flowers. She starts to run."

"You're right!" cries Dara. "She is starting to run."

"She's running to the fence!" shouts Dara's father.

"No, she's not," says Dara. "She's running to the tub."

Dara's father's eyes snap open. "What tub? There isn't any tub in this field."

"There is in my field," says Dara. "And my cow's taking a bath in it."

"A bath?"

"She's very hot," explains Dara. "Because it's such a sunny day. And such a very big field."

"Cows don't take baths," says Dara's father.

"My cows love to bathe," says Dara. "She likes the bubbles best."

"I'm closing my eyes," says Dara.

"Good," says her father. "And do you see the field? Do you see the cows?"

"Yes, I do," says Dara. "I see the cows and they're in the field."

"And what are they doing?"

"They're watching my cow."

"Because she's getting ready to jump over the fence?" asks Dara's father. He sounds hopeful.

"No," says Dara, "because she's swinging."

Dara's father looks at Dara. "She's swinging?"

"From a very big tree," says Dara. "She's drying herself off." Dara giggles. "She forgot to bring a towel."

Dara's father rubs his eyes. "Perhaps if your cow is dry now, we could try just one more time."

"All right," says Dara. She closes her eyes.

"All set?"

"All set," says Dara.

"Your cow has finished drying. She sees that the other cows are waiting for her. They know that she's the best jumper. They won't jump over the fence unless she goes first."

"I see them!" says Dara. "They're all in a line. They're waiting to go."

"And your cow doesn't want to hold them up," says Dara's father. "She's trotting across the field. Faster and faster...

Closer and closer...

Can you see her, Dara? Can you see her getting ready to jump?"

Dara says, "No."

"No?" Dara's father opens his eyes. Dara opens her eyes. "No."

"What do you mean 'No'? Why isn't she getting ready to jump?"

"Because she's looking over the fence," says Dara.

"At what?"

"At the ground," says Dara.

"Whatever for?" asks Dara's father.

"In case it's too far away," says Dara.

"She's not jumping off a cliff, you know," says Dara's father. "She's just jumping over a fence. Now close your eyes and really try to concentrate this time. Your cow is finally getting ready to jump," says Dara's father. "She's galloping across the field. The other cows are following her. Your cow picks up speed... She leaps into the air... Can you see her, Dara? Can you see her leaping?"

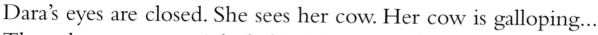

Dara's eyes are closed. She sees her cow. Her cow is galloping...
The other cows are right behind her... Dara's cow leaps into the air...
Dara's father begins to count softly.

"One..." he says.
"One..." says Dara.

"Two..." he says.
"Two..." says Dara.

"Three..." he says.
"Three..." says Dara.

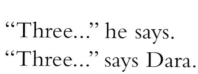

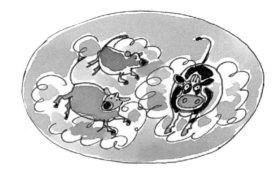

"Zzzz..." he snores.
"Four..." says Dara.

She tiptoes to the window.
"Five...six...seven...
eight...nine..."

SHADOWLAND
Nick Ward

One evening Lily went to bed early. She was hot and uncomfortable and couldn't eat her supper.

Mum brought her a glass of water. "Poor Lily," she said, feeling her brow. "You've got a temperature. Try to sleep for a little while."

Lily played shadow games on the wall. She made a rabbit and a butterfly. Then she made a swan, graceful and proud. When she moved her arm it glided across the wall as if on water; when she wriggled her fingers, it plucked and preened its feathers.

Sleepy now, Lily let her arm fall. But the swan was still there! It spread its wings and cried out. Shapes danced across the wall. A shadow moon rose up over a purple lake. Lily's wall became a shadow land.

Suddenly, the swan reared up and sped across the water.

"Don't go!" cried Lily.

A purple mist swamped Lily's room. Then her bed rose up off the floor and sailed through the wall.

Lily's swan was waiting for her.

The lake became a wild sea. The swan led her over the stormy waves and into a tunnel. Colours danced all around like dreams.

"Mum!" cried Lily. But her voice just echoed around the walls and then away.

Faster and faster they raced through the tunnel and out the other side.

The dream colours tumbled after them,
making flowers and trees and sun and sky.
Lily looked around in wonder. Shadowland
was beautiful.

The lake was now a winding stream. The
swan led Lily on until they came to an island.
Her boat bumped against the grassy shore
and she scrambled out. A path appeared in
the bank and Lily began to climb. When
she looked up, the swan was gone.

The island became a forest, cool and dark.
The further Lily walked the colder it got.
She shivered in her thin nightdress.
When she reached the heart of the forest,
shadowy figures, like little ghosts, came out from
behind the trees and then turned into real live
children. Lily knew they had been waiting for her.

The children joined hands
to keep each other warm.
Dark was falling and the trees
made long shadows across the forest
floor. All night long the children danced
in and out of the trees. They danced through
the night and into the dawn.

Then the forest was gone. Below them a sea of flowers rippled in
the wind. Their heavy scent lifted the children into the air and
tossed them gently about in the clouds. They flew up and up,
right into the heavens.

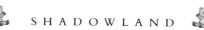

After a while, Lily heard the flapping of wings and out of the clear, bright sky her swan appeared. He had come to take her home. The children flew after him, over hills and mountains and meadows. Lily's arms began to ache. Just as she thought she could go no further, they came to the purple lake. One by one the children fell from the sky and tumbled into the water.

Lily swam down and down until she reached the river bed. She watched the other children turn into silver fishes and dart away through the reeds.

Closing her eyes, Lily let the cool, gentle water wash over her. Her tired limbs felt suddenly light and strong. She spun herself round; a whirlpool caught her and pulled her up to the surface. She thought she could hear someone calling her.

"Lily," said Mum softly.

Lily opened her eyes. She was back in her room. Mum was sitting on her bed.

"You've had a fever," she said. "But it's over now."

Lily smiled.

Outside in the night, a swan swept across the moon as he headed for home... somewhere beyond the shadows.

THE MIDNIGHT DOLL

Maggie Glen

In the darkness of the corner
In its gloomy dusty darkness
Stands Susannah in a cupboard
In a cupboard never opened.

She is old and very fragile
Far too precious to be handled
Standing in her tattered satins
With her hair in matted tresses.

Long ago the one who made her
Made her for a children's playmate.
Oh, how sad they'd be to see her
Lonely, solemn-eyed and dreaming
In the cupboard's dusty darkness.

No small children – no more laughter
Just great-grandma slowly knitting
In the quiet by the fireside
With her needles and their clicking
And the tabby softly purring.

58

Now she sees someone is coming
Skipping, running up the pathway
And behind her comes her mother
Bringing flowers for great-grandma.

Oh, how long the grown-ups chatter
Long throughout the summer evening
Till the shadows grow like giants
Till the little girl grows restless
And she wanders to the corner.

Now Susannah sees her looking
Looking, staring at the cupboard
Sees her climbing upwards to her
Feels those small warm hands around her.

Then great-grandma turns and sees her
Sees her lifting down Susannah
Sees her press her gently to her
Asking, "Was she yours, great-grandma?"
"Yes," great-grandma whispers softly.

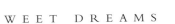

"We must keep her in the cupboard
Though you love her just as I do.
She is old and very fragile
Far too precious to be handled
And we would not wish to harm her."

All too soon the front door closes
And the footstep sounds grow fainter.
Still and silent stands the cottage
Silent as the deepest forest.

Susannah once again is lonely
Sad and lonely in the cupboard
In its dusty gloomy darkness
Only spiders for companions
And the little woodworm beetles.

Deep inside her grows a longing
Grows a longing for a playmate
And Susannah in the cobwebs
Dreams a dream of great adventure.

And the tabby by the fireside
Eyes a-glowing like the embers
Sees the little doll Susannah
Make a knotted rope of ribbons.
Then, with small hands all a-tremble
Clinging to the silken sashes
She is slipping, sliding downwards.

By the door she stands and ponders
Ponders on the moon's great roundness
Sees the vastness of the dark sky
And its blackness pierced with starlight.
All the strangeness of the night-time
Fills the little doll with wonder.

All the little hidden creatures
Hidden deeply in the bushes
Hidden safely in the darkness
Call a shrill and sudden warning

Call, "Oh little doll run swiftly
Hide with us from Moon-faced Hunter
Hide with us among the shadows."

But too late she hears their warning
Hears the whirring of the wing beats
Feels the chill wind of their beating
Feels the talons close around her
Feels the great bird lift her skywards.

High above the park and houses
High above the very tree tops
Flies the fearsome midnight hunter
And Susannah flying with him.

Then she shouts and screams in anger
Screams, "Oh let me go, you monster!"
Screams until the owl is startled
And his deadly talons loosen.

Slowly downwards floats Susannah
Spinning like a leaf in autumn
Till her feet touch something softly
Till she nestles deep in ivy
That fringes round the lighted window.

Warm inside a child is sleeping
Dreaming dreams of times forgotten
Dreams of drowsy summer evenings
And of secret garden places.

Now Susannah with a tapping
Wakens up the little sleeper
Who, while yawning, turns and sees her
At the window, shyly peeping
Lets her in and holds her closely
Filled with happiness at meeting.

On the counterpane by moonlight
Midnight dancing, twirling, leaping
Warmth of far-off times returning
Such a happy, joyful feeling
Susannah and her new friend laughing
Dance and play instead of sleeping.

In the quiet of the sunrise
In the misty grey-blue morning
Comes the moment for returning.
Susannah climbing down the ivy
Hears her new friend softly whisper
"Come back soon, my little dancer."

Small, beneath the giant hedges
Swiftly through the dewy grasses
Susannah running, hurries homeward.

Safely back inside the cupboard
Damp with dewdrops stands Susannah
Stands as she has always stood there
But without a trace of sadness
Just a look that hints at laughter
And a smile that shares a secret
With the tabby by the fireside.

A LETTER TO GRANNY

Paul Rogers and John Prater

Lucy lay in her bed, in her room, in her house, in her street, and thought of the whole town spread out around her.

She fell asleep listening to night noises – distant cars and dogs barking into the dark – and thinking about tomorrow, when Granny would come.

The moment she woke, she knew something was different. Where had all the houses gone? The streets? The town? From her window she could see nothing but sea!

She ran out of the house, barefoot on to the sand – past the garden, past the garage, past the front door, under her own bedroom window.

"Breakfast's ready!" Mum called.

Lucy climbed back up the cliff, leaving a necklace of footprints around the island.

"The postman's late," said Dad.

"I expect the traffic's bad," said Mum.

"I'm going out to watch the whales," said Lucy.

That's where my school used to be, she thought, over there. This is where the road was.

She picked up a starfish. "And there," she laughed, as two crabs scuttled away, "that's where Mr and Mrs Horner lived."

At lunchtime, Lucy told Mum and Dad all about the rock pools, the fish and the sea. But they didn't seem to be listening.

During pudding there was a knock at the door.

"I'll go!" Lucy said.

An enormous liner was anchored off the front garden. On the step stood its captain.

"Pardon me," he said. "I think we're lost. I can't work out where I am."

"This is 101 Acacia Road," said Lucy.

"Ah, thank you," said the captain. "Sorry to trouble you."

After lunch Lucy's parents worked in the garden.
"Look at these lupins!" complained Mum.

"Look at those dolphins!"
called Lucy from the beach.

Suddenly she remembered Granny.
How ever would she get here now?
Someone would have to tell her!
At her toes Lucy saw an old bottle.
She hurried indoors for pen and
paper and wrote:

Dear Granny,
I can't wait to see you.
Our new address is
101 Acacia Road Island.
Please come soon.
Love from Lucy

Then rolling the message up, she
slipped it into the bottle and
pushed it out to sea.

That was when Lucy felt the first drops of rain. The sky grew dark, the sea grew wild, and soon Lucy was hurrying to the house for shelter. From the window she watched the storm.

Now Granny will never make it, she thought.

Then, way out in the distance, she spotted a small boat. One moment it was riding a giant wave, the next it was lost from sight. But gradually it grew bigger and bigger until Lucy could make out her Granny, waving.

"Hello Granny!" she called, running to the water's edge as the rain stopped. Together they climbed the path to the house.

"You look a bit wet," said Dad. "Did you have to wait for the bus?"

After tea, Lucy took Granny
on a tour of the island.
She showed her the crabs
and gulls, the rock pools
and starfish.

"Look," said Granny,
"I've something for you.
Hold it to your ear.
What do you hear?"

So Lucy pressed the warm-coloured, soft-looking, cold, hard shell
to her ear. And in it she heard the sound of the sea.

Then she sat on Granny's lap, on the deckchair, on the beach, on
the island, and together they watched the ripe sun going down.

When it was time for Granny to go,
Lucy waved her goodbye from the
gate. She watched her climbing
into the boat and sailing slowly,
slowly away.

"Time for bed," said Dad.
"I expect Granny will steer by the stars," said Lucy.

That night, Lucy fell asleep listening
to the sighing of the sea and dreaming
all about...

...tomorrow.

LAND OF DREAMS

Michael Foreman

High in the mountains above the jungles, deserts and cities of the world lived an old man and a boy.

They lived in a valley of golden summers and silver streams. In winter everything was covered in a deep blanket of snow. In the higher slopes around the valley it was always winter.

Sometimes great winds blew through the mountains bringing snatches of song and slight traces of sound from the people far below.

The winds also brought fragments of their hopes and dreams, and in the cold mountain air these could just be seen — like breath on a frosty morning.

These fragments would be blown into snowy drifts and remain forever – unfinished dreams and lost hopes among the clouds.

But not quite forgotten. The old man and the boy loved to explore the drifts and uncover the dreams.

They would push and pull them into their valley, which became a vast store of bits and pieces. A scrapyard of dreams.

Sometimes pieces could be fitted together, and the old man and the boy would build and build. On warm days the entire collection would disappear, only to re-appear in the cold night air.

The old man and the boy worked well together, and between them could solve most of the puzzles.

When they had completed the shape of a dream they sent it sliding off down the mountain to the warmer air where it would become invisible once more and drift around the world and make people smile without knowing why.

Then one day a giant wandered into the valley. He was very sad.

"I've been a giant for a thousand years," he moaned to the old man and the boy. "In the old days it was great. I used to stomp about in the dreams of everyone. Now no one thinks of me. Earthquakes, thunder and natural disasters get all the credit."

"Can we be of any help?" asked the boy.

"No one can help a giant," said the giant with a great sigh that caused an avalanche at the end of the valley revealing more buried dreams.

"But you can be a big help to us," cried the old man. "Stay awhile and rest."

So the giant made himself a shelter from the rubble of dreams, and marvelled at the way it disappeared on warm sunny days but always returned to protect him from the cold.

After a while, the giant began to help his new friends with their work, taking some of the most interesting pieces of dream to embellish and extend his home.

With the giant's help, really big pieces could be recovered and assembled and sent off skidding and disappearing into the world.

Then, one day, they discovered that the top five hundred feet of the highest mountain was in fact the rubble of a massive dream.

There was no room in the valley for such a big dream, so they had to piece it together in the swirling mist and snow. It was so enormous they could not see the overall shape.

After many hours it was finished.

The boy, the old man, and the giant moved to one end of the dream and pushed. Slowly the dream began to move, then slid faster and faster.

Suddenly, the giant raced after the dream and leapt aboard.

The dream and the giant shot out of the mist and could be seen quite clearly before they vanished into the clouds below, the giant shouting joyfully, "Now they will remember me!"

The old man and the boy returned to their valley. The giant had found his dream.

"Perhaps, one day," said the old man, "you will find your dream, and follow it far from here."

"But I've *found* my dream," said the boy as the mountains slowly vanished in the warmth of his bed and he turned over smiling without knowing why.

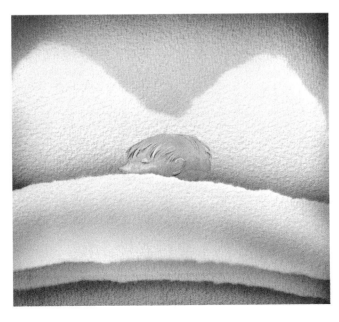

THE MAGPIE AND THE STAR

Stephen Lambert

This story began one night – when nights were not quite as they are now. Then, the moon shone full and round, all night and every night.

A time came, however, when the moon felt tired and decided to take a rest. Before doing so, she made a number of stars to shine in her place. The brightest star settled above a hill. Beneath the hill lived Pol.

Now, Pol was a solitary fellow. He lived by himself and for himself. He mistrusted the world outside, and although he had made a beautiful garden, a thick hedge ran around it so he alone could enjoy its fruits.

No visitors ever set foot inside – even the travelling folk somehow knew that in this place no welcome was to be had.

At night, Pol would watch the moon casting its light over his garden. One evening, however, he looked out and gasped in astonishment. The moon had vanished from the sky! In its place shone a single star. Its light touched the edge of the hill and its smile caught the corners of his mouth.

Pol felt in his heart that this brilliant star was a gift for him alone, and as time passed he began to love it and to treasure it above all things.

But Pol was not the only one to be captivated. From a tree high above the house, a magpie watched. He saw how Pol cherished the star and by his own greedy nature began to desire it for himself.

One night he flew down into the garden and spoke to Pol,

"I've a sparkling pile of treasure in my nest," he said. "Give me the star and it can all be yours."

"Off with you, magpie!" cried Pol, angrily. "All you see around you belongs to me, including the hill and the sky above."

"Well, what won't be given can be easily
taken," screeched the magpie and with
that he flew up into the black night,
seized the star and was gone!

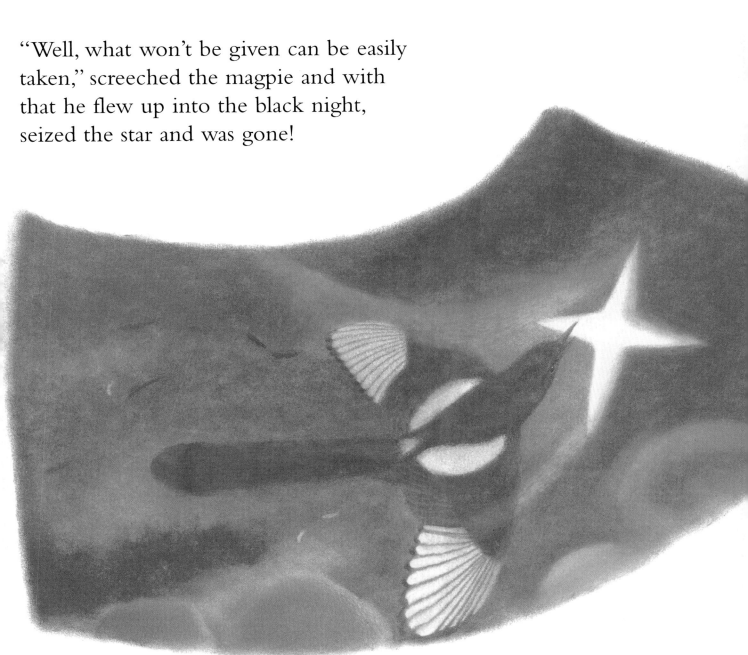

Days passed. Pol began to mourn, and could neither eat nor sleep
for thinking of the star. Then, one morning, he made up his mind
to search for it. When he found it he would keep it for himself.

He set off at once, climbing the hill to meet the sky where the
star had once shone.

When he reached the top he found himself at the foot of an orange tree – its branches bowed over by the weight of countless oranges.

"Have you seen the magpie who stole the star?" demanded Pol.

The tree sighed. "I know that bird," it said, "for I heard it screech as it flew over. But my face was bent to the ground and where he flew I cannot tell. However, if you could only shake this fruit from my branches I will do what I can for you."

Pol hesitated, but he did as he was asked and when the last orange had fallen, the tree told Pol to break off one of its branches.

"This is my gift," said the orange tree. "It may be of use to you in your search."

Pol stepped on
his way and
after a while he
came to a pool.
Beside it was
a heron, and
drawing closer
Pol saw that
one of its wings
was broken.

"Have you
seen the magpie
who stole the
star?" he asked.

"I know that
wicked bird,"
replied the
heron. "But I
cannot think
while this wing
gives me such
pain. Two crows

came after my eggs and my wing was broken as I beat them off. If
only you would help me, then I may be able to help you in return."

So Pol broke the branch and in a moment had made a splint
which he gently bound to the bird's wing.

The heron thanked him, and from her nest she pulled a long,
green reed which she gave to Pol. "This is my gift," she said, "and
who knows, maybe it will help you find what you're looking for."

Pol followed the path until he came to a river. On the bank sat a
fisherman with a net draped over his knees.

"Have you seen the magpie who stole the star?" asked Pol.

However the fisherman didn't seem to hear him. "What a day!"
he sighed. "How can I possibly catch anything with this gaping
hole in my net?"

"Take this," said Pol, and he handed him the long green reed.
At once the fisherman threaded it through a wooden needle, and
before you could say "Pike!" had mended his net. Then he put his
hand in his pocket and took out a large swan mussel. Inside was
a perfect pearl.

"This is my gift," said the fisherman. "Take it to the highest of
those three hills you see in the distance; when night falls, lay it on
the ground and wait. That greedy magpie
will soon catch sight of it and be
unable to resist. Be careful,
though, do not give it up
until he tells you where
the star is to be found."

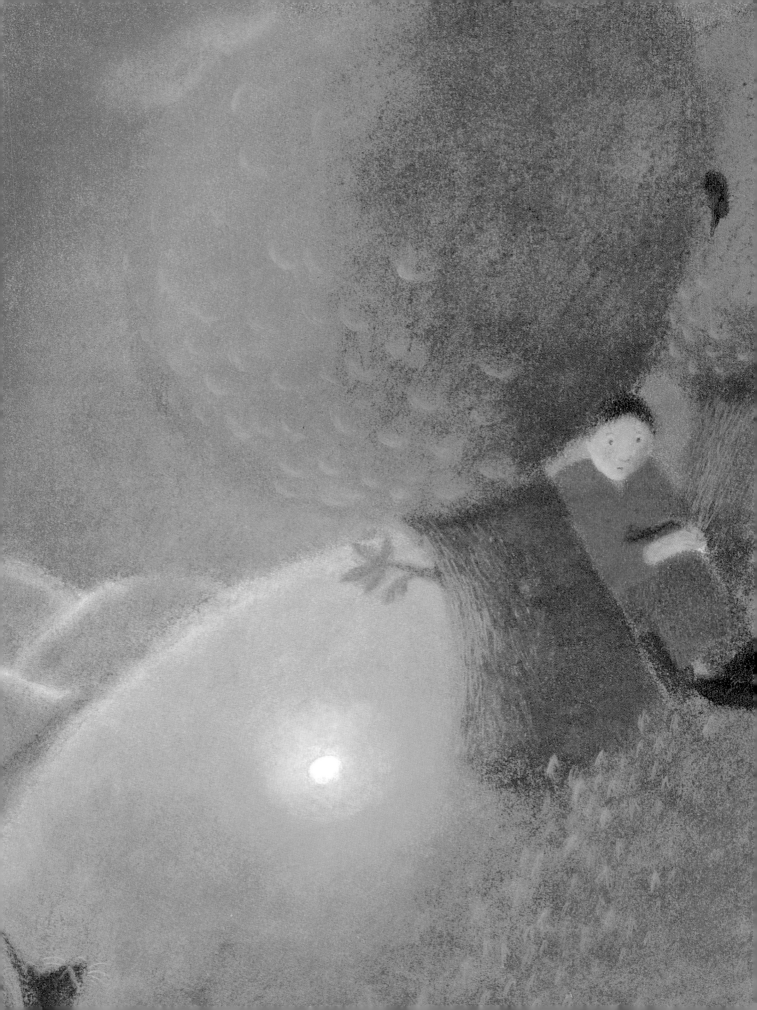

Pol was weary, but still he journeyed on – on and up to the top of the highest hill and there he placed the pearl. Then he hid behind a tree and waited until the sky grew dark.

Then, out of nowhere came the sudden beating of wings. Down swooped the magpie and made to snatch up the pearl.

"Not so fast!" cried Pol. "First you must tell me where you have hidden the star."

Now, the magpie badly wanted the pearl and thought how he could best make a bargain without really giving the secret away. He began:

"No hand can reach her though green fingers caress her.
Hidden from view and curtained in blue.
On a bed she lies but no blanket hides."

When the magpie had finished, Pol was obliged to hand over the pearl and the trickster flew off, greatly pleased with himself.

Pol tried to make sense of the riddle, but the day had been long and he soon fell asleep.

Whether they really came or if it was all in a dream, Pol never knew. But first he heard the fisherman speak to him:

"The star lies in water. The green fingers are the reeds that caress her."

Next he heard the heron:

"Look for the deepest pool in the river where the water is darkest blue and even I, with my long neck, cannot reach the bottom."

Lastly, from its hill far away, the whisper of the orange tree came to Pol:

"Remember how I was bowed over by the weight of my fruit? Well, fill your pockets with stones and they will carry you down to where the star lies hidden. When you have found her, empty your pockets and you will rise safely to the surface."

When Pol awoke he remembered all that he had heard, and set off to the river. He paused at every pool but all were too shallow. At last, he came to a pool so deep and so dark that below the surface he could see nothing but blackness.

Pol filled his pockets as the orange tree had told him and taking a deep breath, plunged into the water.

Down, down he sank, a soft light guiding him to the water's icy depths. Suddenly, the light grew brighter, and there on the river bed lay the star. Pol's heart was filled with joy.

Quickly, he picked up the star, tumbled the stones from his pockets and rose swiftly to the surface.

Pol stood on the river bank and held the star before him. Now, at last, it was his to keep forever. Then Pol started. He thought of the orange tree, the heron and the fisherman, and how he had given and been rewarded with kindness.

The star shone as if all the light of the moon was within it. Pol raised his arms and let it go. It soared up into the blue night, its luminous trail leaving behind a sweetly curved arc.

"This is *my* gift," said Pol.

Then he turned homewards, to his house and the garden that awaited him.

Above, in the sky, hung the star. It shone above the land below, over the orange tree, the heron and the fisherman, and over Pol.

THE GARDEN
Dyan Sheldon and Gary Blythe

Jenny found a stone while she was digging in the garden. It was dark and rough and came to a point. She had never seen anything quite like it before.

"Look at this," said Jenny. "I think it must be a magic stone."

Jenny's mother smiled. "That's not a magic stone. It's a flint." She touched it with her finger. "It might even be an arrowhead. It could be hundreds of years old."

Jenny looked around the garden. There were beds of flowers against the fence, and a fish pond in one corner. In the middle of the lawn there were a swing set and a barbecue. Beyond the garden there were houses and street lights and busy roads; and beyond them the stores of the town and the buildings of the city.

"What was it like here hundreds of years ago?" asked Jenny.

Her mother took the stone and turned it over in her hand.

"There were none of the things you see here now," she said.

Jenny stared beyond the garden, but it was hard to imagine what it must have been like when there were forests instead of cities, and fields instead of towns.

But then, far in the distance, Jenny saw a man on horseback, looking as though he might ride into the clouds. She blinked and the man disappeared.

Jenny turned back to her mother. "I thought I saw an Indian brave just then," she told her. "He was crossing the plains on his pony."

Jenny's mother handed her the piece of flint and they talked of how the world had been when the land was large and as open as the sky, of hunting on the plains and in the mountains and forests, of singing, and telling stories in the firelight.

"There's little left of that way of life now," her mother sighed.

"There's still my arrowhead," said Jenny.

"Yes," agreed her mother. "There's still your arrowhead."

Jenny stayed in the garden all afternoon. She tried to imagine people walking with their dogs and riding their horses across the faraway hills.

But all she saw were cars and trucks racing along the busy road.

She tried to picture young men hunting in the high grass of the plains, their movements slow and their weapons ready.

But all she saw was the cat stalking through the flowers and her mother's shrubs.

As dusk blurred the shapes in the garden, Jenny almost thought she heard women bent over their fires, their voices soft and laughing.

But it was only the radio in the house next door.

Jenny was still outside when the moon came up.

"Jenny!" called her mother from the house. "Come on in, it's getting dark."

But Jenny pretended not to hear. She wanted to stay where she was, watching in the garden.

Later, she asked if she could sleep in her tent, the way people used to. Jenny's mother sighed.

"All right," she said. "But we must put your tent close to the house so I can keep an eye on you."

Jenny lay awake for a long time that night. She listened for the howling of the wolves and gazed out at the stars. She stared at the sky so hard that she thought she saw a trail of clouds turn into buffalo and race across the moon. When finally she did fall asleep, the arrowhead was still fast in her hand.

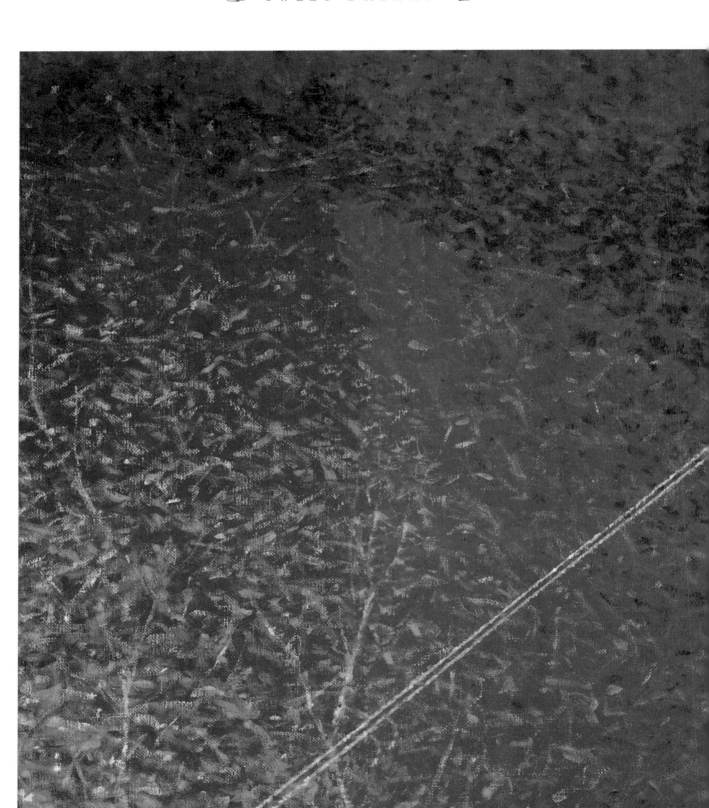

Jenny had a dream. She dreamt that she woke in the night.
From somewhere close by came the murmur of low voices.

She cautiously opened the flap of her tent.
The world outside had changed.

The moon was corn-yellow and the stars sat low in a blue-black sky.

There were no houses or lights, no roads and no cars. Where the city had been there were only hills. Where the town had stood were fields of grass. Night birds called and the trees rustled. Jenny's garden was gone.

She looked around in wonder. There were ponies where the vegetable patch should have been, and dogs dozing where the flowers had grown. In place of the fish pond was a whispering stream. Instead of the swing set, painted tipis stood in a clearing, smoke drifting past them like clouds. And there, where the barbecue had been, a circle of people sat round a fire, their voices soft.

One of the men turned and looked towards Jenny. He beckoned her over.

Because it was a dream, Jenny knew what he wanted. He wanted her to return his stone.

The dogs began to bark as Jenny crawled from her tent, but because she was dreaming she wasn't afraid. She crossed to the fire.

The man moved over and Jenny sat down. She placed the arrowhead into his hand.

Jenny sat with the Indians all through the night, while the drum played, and the flute sounded, and they told her how the world had been, so long ago, when the land was large. When there were stories in the stars and songs in the sun. When every thing on earth had a voice and a heart, and time was measured by the changings of the moon.

In the morning, when Jenny really woke up, the world was as it always was again. The flowers were still growing along the fence. The cars were still speeding past on the busy road. The arrowhead was still in her hand.

Jenny stared beyond the yard. Clouds drifted past the sun like smoke. The beating of her heart recalled the drumming of her dream.

Without a sound, Jenny crept from her tent. At the edge of the garden she knelt in the grass, and buried the arrowhead back in the earth.

She looked up at the sky. And just for an instant, in the shimmering light, she saw the world as it once was, so long ago, when the land was large.

LULLABY
Shirley Hughes

Time for sleep, time to rest,
Snuggle in your woolly nest.
Let me safely tuck you in,
Dark without, warm within.

Far away, train whistles call,
Car lights sweep the nursery wall,
Muffled footsteps passing by,
A quiet moon in a quiet sky.

Soft blanket, smooth sheet,
Tuck the quilt around your feet,
Close your eyes and I will keep
A watch beside you while you sleep.

Acknowledgements

THE PUBLISHERS GRATEFULLY ACKNOWLEDGE PERMISSION TO REPRODUCE THE
FOLLOWING STORIES, WHICH ARE PUBLISHED IN LONGER, COMPLETE EDITIONS
BY ANDERSEN PRESS LTD, 20 VAUXHALL BRIDGE ROAD, LONDON SW1V 2SA:

The Midnight Feast © text Lindsay Camp 1996 © illustrations Tony Ross 1996

Land of Dreams © Michael Foreman 1982

THE PUBLISHERS GRATEFULLY ACKNOWLEDGE AUTHORS AND ILLUSTRATORS
OF BOOKS PUBLISHED UNDER THEIR OWN IMPRINTS AS FOLLOWS:

My Blanket is Blue, published by Hutchinson Children's Books,
© Hilda Offen 1998

The Dreambeast, published by Hutchinson Children's Books,
© John Richardson 1988

Counting Cows, published by Hutchinson Children's Books,
© text Dyan Sheldon 1994 © illustrations Wendy Smith 1994

Shadowland, published by Hutchinson Children's Books,
© Nick Ward 1993

The Midnight Doll, published by Hutchinson Children's Books,
© Maggie Glen 1996

A Letter to Granny, published by The Bodley Head,
© text Paul Rogers 1994 © illustrations John Prater 1994

The Magpie and the Star, published by Hutchinson Children's Books,
© Stephen Lambert 1991

The Garden, published by Hutchinson Children's Books,
© text Dyan Sheldon 1993 © illustrations Gary Blythe 1993
Thanks also to Viking, US

Lullaby, published by The Bodley Head in *Rhymes for Annie Rose*,
© Shirley Hughes 1995